JUNCTURES

THE BEATITUDES ILLUSTRATED THROUGH STORIES OF CRISES

MARK ANDRLIK

Charleston, SC
www.PalmettoPublishing.com

Junctures
Copyright © 2022 by Mark Andrlik

Paperback ISBN: 979-8-88590-478-0
eBook ISBN: 979-8-88590-479-7

ACKNOWLEDGEMENT

With gratitude to my wife, Evette, and daughter, Kamyla,
for their generous contribution of time and wisdom.
Also, to Bill, Carol, Jimmy, and Scott.

Juncture:
- A point of time, especially one made critical or important by a concurrence of circumstances
- A serious state of affairs; crisis

~ dictionary.com

CONTENTS

JENNIFER
1

TODD
27

EZRA
53

MILES
75

JONATHAN
97

CALVIN
121

THE STANHOPE FAMILY
141

FRAN
165

JENNIFER

Throbbing pain and the world spinning; stomach in knots, even after brief relief from vomiting. Minutes passed and the spinning eased off. Drifting clouds obscured the moon, casting the land in cold darkness, save the glow of a brightly lit rectangle a way off.

"Where am I?" Jennifer Partridge spoke to no one. A breath of wind and the rustling of tall grasses answered. She raised herself up onto one elbow and rotated her aching head to get a better look at the light. It was a billboard. She blinked and squinted until the sign came into focus—the image of a woman's smiling face and the words "Your Dream Home is Waiting," followed by a name and a phone number. A real estate agent's ad.

My dream home? Very funny! I'm happy where I live now.

Where was her jacket? She held her position for several minutes, waiting for another wave of nausea to pass before attempting to move further.

Her forehead felt wet. She lifted her right hand to touch it. Was that blood? Mixed with mascara? Great! Where else was she hurt? There were scrapes along her right forearm and elbow, and her lower back ached, but she could move her arms and legs; evidently no broken bones.

Where am I, and how did I get here?

A breeze arose, bringing goosebumps to bare arms, but also a welcomed coolness to her face, relieving feelings of nausea. She needed her jacket. And her backpack. Where were they?

A distant hum from behind steadily crescendoed into a roar; a pickup truck plowed past, spewing diesel fumes, and stirring up bits of dirt that pelted her face.

The jerk! Why hadn't he stopped?

No wonder. She was sprawled among clumps of grass on the shoulder of a blacktop road and dressed in dark clothing—like a black garbage bag, unnoticeable to any driver who wasn't specifically watching for a human being. She struggled to a sitting position and rotated her head to look around. Bleak, lonely darkness, save the dwindling taillights of the pickup truck. And the billboard.

Was that music? Led Zeppelin's "Stairway to Heaven"? No. Nothing but a faint breath of wind all around. But the screeching voice and driving guitar licks persisted—*a memory*, emerging with visions of low lighting and muffled voices in gloomy space. Coming into focus. The odors of cooking grease and beer. A small round tabletop.

Then… sudden clarity. *Razor!* The tall, pale-skinned, heavily tattooed man with a shaved head, goatee, and a long scar on his neck had approached her the moment they made eye contact in Pfenninger's Pub in South Minneapolis. The reputed kingpin of a gang of south Minneapolis drug dealers who, according to legend, had received his signature scar from an opponent's straight razor in a fight. A fight in which he had prevailed, wrestling the blade from his foe, thereby earning the respect of his peers and his new name.

Razor, who had earlier this evening—was it only this evening? How long had she been out? —taken a place at her table and ordered drinks, was the subject of the feature story that Jennifer was determined to publish in the *Gazette*, further advancing her reputation as the reporter willing to step out and take risks where others in her profession wouldn't. The initial thrill of the capture at his approach was encouraged by his friendly disposition and the nature of their small talk. She had been ready to take the leap of inquiring into the man's life, his background, motives, vision for his life, but then he had shut it all down…

Rubbing her forearms for warmth, Jennifer stood. Unsteady at first, she eventually regained sufficient equilibrium to further survey her surroundings. Newly planted rows of corn lining both sides of the highway; the billboard; and a faint row of lights on the horizon, possibly an outlying subdivision. Another draught of cool air and Jennifer remembered her belongings. After another look around, she located her jacket nearby, sprinkled with dirt and gravel. She shook it out and gratefully pulled it on. Now, to find her backpack, the pack that held her files, her laptop, cellphone, wallet, and other personal items.

Where was it? Fighting back panic, Jennifer paced about in ever-widening circles, looking for her pack.

Gone.

That's when the distant headlights of an approaching vehicle appeared. Jennifer stepped to the middle of the highway and raised both arms.

"Again? We've already been through this." Jennifer massaged both temples with her fingertips in a vain attempt to ease the nagging pain. The gash on her forehead had been cleaned and bandaged, but dull aches lingered in her back and shoulders, with little relief provided by the pain reliever the ER nurse had given her two hours earlier. Those conditions were not helped by several hours of sitting in waiting rooms, along with invasive questioning by both medical and law enforcement personnel.

"Yep, we have. But we're going through it once more. Maybe twice. Might pick up something we missed earlier. You're not exactly at your best, you know." Officer Chad Burns rubbed his eyes with both hands, stifled a yawn, then scooted his chair back from the small conference table.

The young officer, probably in his mid-thirties, had treated Jennifer kindly when he picked her up from Hennepin County General, seeming to have a gift for handling trauma victims with compassion and respect. But his manner was becoming short, almost gruff. "This hasn't exactly been a picnic for me either, you know. More coffee?"

"Thanks." Despite her own situation, she did sympathize with the man. He probably had a wife and children sleeping at home while he dealt with the late-night messes of people in trouble. And he looked tired himself, no doubt having been on shift for several hours prior to dealing with her.

Burns stepped over to where a half-filled carafe rested on its burner, the unpleasant odor of burned coffee permeating their small quarters. Nevertheless, Jennifer accepted another refill, bitter and served up in a Styrofoam cup. Her dry throat welcomed the hot liquid.

Burns returned to his seat across the table and handed her the cup. A reversal of roles. She, the reporter, would normally be in his position, sizing up her subject and asking the questions. Movements and facial expressions and offhand comments would be observed and noted. Except that this time she herself was the subject.

Jennifer took a sip, then arched her back and rotated both shoulders in a vain attempt to ease the aches. Twenty-five years old and in good physical condition, she was accustomed to the pains and bruises that accompanied rigorous workouts or physical sporting activities. But tonight's series of events had introduced kinds of pain that she hadn't before encountered.

By her own calculations, she figured that she had been unconscious for at least a couple of hours, likely from a drug. Had she been bumped about during that time? Stuffed into the trunk of Razor's car? Even pushed out of a moving vehicle?

The stiff, straight-backed chair in which she sat facing Officer Burns offered no comfort. Nor did the sterile surroundings of the small conference room in the south Minneapolis police precinct building where she had spent the last portion of a long night. What must it feel like to put in long overnight work shifts in such a place? Perhaps an interview with Officer Burns himself would be of interest to her readers. Something to consider.

But, despite her discomfort, Jennifer did not express any hint of regret over her decisions which had precipitated her present circumstance. Given the chance, she would do it all again, albeit more cautiously.

"Tell me again." Burns sipped twice-baked coffee and picked up his pen. "What happened tonight? From start to finish. Every detail."

"Uh, okay." Jennifer tugged at her hair and took another sip from her cup. She'd rather go home to a hot shower, then fall into bed and hope for sleep. But she was at Officer Burns's mercy at present.

"It was about seven o'clock. I was sitting at a table with Razor at Pfenninger's. I had caught his eye right away when he walked into the place, and he came right over to me. He was by himself and appeared to be in a good enough mood. Polite; not high or drunk or anything like that. We made small talk for a few minutes, and he bought me a drink. Actually, two. Things were going smoothly. He seemed to be enjoying my company."

"Did you leave the table at any time while he sat there?"

"No. And neither did he. And no one talked to us or bothered us. The place was fairly quiet."

"Did you take your eyes off Razor at any time? Were you ever distracted?"

"No… uh" —a new nugget came to light in her memory— "maybe once. When my phone went off down in my backpack. I had it on the floor between my feet, and I dug around in it long enough to check on who was calling. But I didn't take the call."

"How long did that effort take? How long were you bent down, eyes off Razor?"

"Maybe twenty seconds?"

"Okay." Burns scribbled more notes.

"We talked for a while longer."

"How much longer?"

"Hmm. Maybe ten or fifteen minutes."

"And you finished your second drink?"

"Yes."

More notetaking. Burns nodded for her to continue.

"Then he said he needed to leave and offered to walk me to my car. We both stepped outside and started down the sidewalk toward where I had parked. I have no idea what happened after that, but the next thing I knew, I woke up on the side of the road."

"And back before you left the pub, had you begun your interview? You know, asking Razor questions, questions which he may have considered invasive?"

"Barely. Like I said, it was mostly chit-chat. About the local social scene and so forth."

"Had you told him who you were? And what you were doing?"

"Just getting to that. I was segueing into my interview mode when he stopped me."

"Why? Did he get a phone call? Did someone else show up?"

"No. He looked at his phone and told me he needed to leave."

"And you agreed to leave with him?"

"Yes, he insisted on walking me to my car, close by out front. I had no intention of anything beyond that. I had hoped to schedule a future meeting with him, or at least get his phone number, but obviously that never happened."

"And you're certain that you had your backpack with you when you left?"

"Yes, slung over my right shoulder, like always."

"And about what time would you guess you and Razor left?"

"Sorry. I don't know. Maybe seven-thirty or eight?"

"Then let me get this straight, Jennifer." Burns looked at her sternly. "You're determined to do a feature story about Razor for your newspaper, so you set yourself up to interview him about himself and his lifestyle and his operations—all while hoping he would be okay with that?"

"Yes, that was the idea. You see, guys like that have pride, bravado. They enjoy the attention and the press. Anything that doesn't incriminate of course. I have to think that he'd be pleased to be featured."

Burns stopped, set down his pen, and stared at her, the expression on his face a mixture of concern, admiration, and incredulity. "Based on your account of everything, I'd say you're lucky to be alive, with nothing more than a bump on the head and an upset stomach. Do you realize who you're dealing with in Razor?"

"I've done my homework."

"In that case." Burns leaned back and rubbed his eyes. "I'd have to say that you've either lost your mind or else you have a death wish. Razor is not a man to be toyed with. Nothing is out of bounds for him. He's dangerous. Amoral. No concept of right and wrong."

Anger flared. "Amoral? No sense of right and wrong?" She glared at Burns, her present circumstances momentarily forgotten. "What does that mean? Razor is a human being, no different than you or me. He has his own point of view, his own way of looking at the world. I don't judge the man. I have no idea of what he's been through in life or how he thinks. That's why I find him so fascinating. Hence, the feature article. His story needs to be told."

Burns betrayed no reaction to her outburst other than a tightening of his jaw. "Well, have it your way. But I'm telling you that he's dangerous and slippery. We have a history with the man to prove it. Tell me this. If he were holding a razor blade to your throat, would you still be inclined not to judge him? Huh?"

"You're talking 'what-ifs.' I deal with reality."

"Okay, but reality this time is that he likely drugged your drink. Probably slipped it in when you were down digging around for your phone. Then he kept track of the time from when you finished your drink, escorted you outside before you lost consciousness, and somehow got you into his own car without drawing attention."

"I suppose any witnesses could have thought I was drunk."

"Maybe, but I doubt it. More likely, if anyone that saw you knew Razor, they would have known to steer clear and keep their mouth shut. People that know him fear him. We'll know more about if and how he drugged you when we get your lab results."

"But let's consider Razor's point of view in this situation." Jennifer sat up straight, her reporter instincts awakened. "Why did he do what he did tonight? You know, drug me, haul me off, and dump me out on the road—all without violating me, if you know what I mean? Was his only motive the theft of my stuff?"

"Whew! Who knows the motives of a guy like that? Maybe, initially, he hit on you and bought you a drink for the usual reasons. Then he felt you were asking too many questions and changed his plans. Decided to knock you out. To punish you, to scare you off for good. Or to take you back to his place and have his way with you. But, for some reason which I can't understand, he didn't do either, although he apparently did hang on to your pack. All in all, I'm quite amazed that you got out of this as well as you have."

Burns lobbed his empty coffee cup into a wastebasket and stretched his arms. "Jennifer, I must confess. I can't quite figure how you think. You knew that you were walking into a potentially life-threatening situation."

"Sure. It can be the best way to get information. So, yes, I went into this thing eyes wide open."

"And did your editor send you out to interview Razor?"

"Oh, no. John would never ask that. But he appreciates that I bring him the tips and the stories that no other reporter can seem to get."

"But this time, instead of snagging a good story you get abducted. You're here at the station with a bandage on your head. Picked up on the road by some kind stranger and dropped off at Hennepin County General ER at about ten-fifteen. That means you were out cold for about a couple of hours. Then brought here in my squad car at two in the morning and subjected to more questioning and paperwork. All with your vital personal possessions stolen." Burns looked up at the clock on the wall. "It's nearly four o'clock. I'm going to drive you home to where your roommate is graciously waiting up for you. How's that for a great ending to your escapade?"

"Not what I had hoped for, obviously."

"Jennifer, you didn't get your story, but you should be gratful. In my opinion, Razor did you a favor by merely robbing you and dumping you off like a bag of trash. Things could have been much worse."

Stepping through the entrance of the long brick building which housed the offices of the *Gazette,* Jennifer experienced a premonition of her editor's mood, even through the fog which lingered in her brain. It was well before operating hours and the building was still empty, except for one office at the far end of the hall. Her awareness of John's state of mind grew stronger with each hollow-sounding tap of her steps on the tile floor. She knocked on his half-open door.

"Come in, Jen." He clipped his words. Her editor, a stocky, middle-aged man with blond hair, bright blue eyes, and a normally ruddy complexion, looked pale and worn. The look on his face confirmed what she had felt earlier. Without speaking, he motioned for her to take a seat. She dutifully complied, awaiting the expected tirade.

"Jen, we've had this discussion before." John's voice shook, and he repeatedly clicked the ink pen clutched in his trembling right hand. "I'm this close to firing you, for your own good. Your own safety." He made a pinching gesture with the index finger and thumb of his other hand and glared at her.

"So you've told me. More times than I can count." Her response was flat, emotionless. She didn't care, having gotten home less than two hours earlier with a headache and upset stomach, and no sleep after that.

"But no one—I mean no one! —in my employ ever goes out and puts themselves in danger the way you did last night. You have known that from the start. What am I to do with you? Not only have you gone out and nearly gotten yourself raped or killed, but you've lost a boatload of confidential and vital information. If Razor is smart enough to get past our password security, then the identities of many of the *Gazette's* news sources could be compromised. Not to mention your personal private information."

"Yes, I know," she replied sheepishly. The potential breach of security was unfortunate, but that was part of the risk in chasing down a story. "But it would take a top-notch hacker to get through our security. Someone way out of Razor's league. He deals in illegal drugs, not technology."

John sighed. "You'd better be right about that. Officer Burns expressed similar concerns during the phone call he placed to me in the wee hours last night to inform me of all the gory details—followed by twenty minutes of questioning about your character and habits. How did you even manage to get to work this morning?"

"Sorry about that. I would have called you myself but Burns insisted. As for my getting here, my roommate dropped me off on her way to work."

"You look like a train wreck." John rubbed his eyes. "Frankly, I'm feeling about the same way that you look. Not much sleep for me either after that. My wife wasn't too thrilled with the late phone call either."

"Sorry."

"Jen, you've been watching too much CSI or other television drama. Your attitude and your methods are simply wrong at times. We're running a newspaper here, not the FBI."

Jennifer's hackles rose. "No, it's not wrong. It's called aggressive journalism. It's risky, but I get the job done."

"No, it's wrong. There's a right way to get a story and a wrong way."

"I beg to differ. There is no right or wrong. There is, however, something called doing my job, and doing it better than anyone else, and getting the best stories for our paper. While every other paper in town is consumed with the I-35 bridge collapse, or the crashes of commercial airliners in other parts of the world, the *Gazette* brings something different to our reading public. My feature stories do generate interest and comments; you cannot deny that!"

He seemed to soften. "Jen, you know I value your hard work and dedication to our profession. You are a loyal employee and an excellent reporter. But you're a renegade when it comes to stuff like this. What drives you?"

"Oh, the usual. More money. More power and responsibility, not to mention the acclaim. That's never been a secret. You know that I can't resist a challenge, and this profession offers plenty."

"Granted. But what about a moral code? Do you have parameters within which you think and operate?"

"What do you mean?" Her defensive instincts quickened. John was not above challenging her world view with his own distorted ideas.

"In other words, do you have any sense of what is right versus wrong? Ethical versus unethical?"

"John, don't go down that universal law path with me again. I don't want to hear any more about absolutes, about the law of gravity, or our assurance that the sun will rise every morning."

"Okay. Then… what *is* your code?"

"Don't have one and don't need one like you describe. I do understand that my decisions and actions have consequences. That reality was very clearly demonstrated last night. But those are simply that: my decisions and their consequences. Within my own control. My own business."

"Well, I don't agree with your line of reasoning, but at least you seem to take responsibility for yourself."

"Exactly. I'm beholden to no one and take care of myself."

His tired expression wilted further. "Okay, I'll allow that you do look out for yourself… most of the time. Not last night."

"No. I'll admit that."

"But think about what you've told me. Your careless comment about not being beholden to anyone but yourself is simply not true. And let me remind you that you are beholden to me when it comes to your job. Don't you dare pull any more stunts like this with me."

Several sharp raps sounded at the door.

"Who's there?" Jennifer called out, slipping her breakfast dishes into the sink. The clock on the stove showed 7:33 AM. Her room-mate had long ago left for work. Who would this be?

"It's Officer Burns. From the precinct."

"Oh!" She crossed the room and pulled the door open.

Burns, looking considerably more rested, held out her back-pack on outstretched arms. "Sorry for the unannounced visit, but I couldn't call ahead, for obvious reasons."

"You've got my backpack. Sweet!"

"Yes. In accordance with protocol, we've gone through it thor-oughly. It does appear that everything is here, per the inventory you gave me the other night. Look for yourself."

"Wow! Thanks! Come on in, and I'll have a peek at it. Here." Feeling giddy over this unexpected turn of fortune, she pointed to a box on the counter. "You're a cop, right? You must need a doughnut. It's the least I can do since you brought my pack over."

"Very funny." Burns wasn't laughing.

Her quick inspection of her pack located all its expected con-tents: cellphone, laptop, wallet, books, and a bundle of paper files. Even her credit cards and the currency in the wallet. Other than a few dirt smudges, the pack looked the way she had last carried it two nights earlier.

"Everything's still here. Amazing! I'm thrilled."

"Well, don't be too thrilled. There's more to the story."

"Oh? Where did you find this?"

"Not in good place. There was a shooting at an apartment early yesterday morning, not too far from here. All the signs of a drug deal gone bad. One man dead at the scene. Two others arrested, both bad news. Guys we've been chasing for some time."

"Sorry to hear that, but glad you caught those guys. But what does that have to do with my backpack?"

"It was there."

"What, my backpack? Where? At the scene of the shooting?"

"Yes, I'm afraid so. Sitting on a chair right in the same room where everything went down. You're lucky it doesn't have blood spatters on it."

"Oh."

"It was removed and inventoried along with everything else in that space. Our crime lab has gone through it, fingerprinted everything. No fingerprints or anything else of use to our investigation. I had already reported it stolen, so it was returned to me late yesterday."

"Did they get Razor? Was he there?"

"No, but I'm not surprised. The guy is smart enough to not get caught. But he obviously had been with those guys at some point—either before or after he got rid of you."

"Ooh." A sobering possibility. "Do you think he pulled the trigger?"

"We don't know. No gun was found. Neither of the men in custody has been pegged as the shooter. And they're not talking."

Jennifer let out a long breath and slumped down onto a chair.

Burns looked troubled. "The fact that your pack was in their possession puts you at risk—way beyond the risk you knew you were taking by meeting with Razor in the first place. Razor knows a lot of thugs, and we don't know who all was there. Any one of them could have gone through your stuff."

"True. What can I do about all of this?"

"Well," Burns sighed. "Identity theft is not our primary concern in this case. Drug addicts are typically not into that, at least not the bunch picked up yesterday. But you'll still need to take some measures to protect yourself in that regard. Watch your accounts, change passwords, and so on."

"Okay."

"Interestingly, they hadn't taken your currency, so there is some hope that they hadn't even opened your pack. But the fact that Razor had contact with these individuals right on the heels of your own encounter with him concerns me. Along with the fact that you were unconscious for a couple of hours."

"Am I a suspect?"

"That's one thing you don't have to worry about. This all went down at the same time we were having our little chat at the station, and I had reported your pack as stolen by that time. You have an alibi."

"So, what happens?"

"There's nothing for you to do right now. But remain alert. Razor knows who you are and where you live and work. You do understand the implications of that, don't you?"

"Oh, yes."

"Then, let's deal with what we can. How about your car? You've got your keys. I can give you a lift to go pick it up."

"Oh, it's here. I keep a second set of keys here, and my roommate took me over to pick it up yesterday."

"Good enough." Burns tipped his cap. "In that case, I've got to run, but don't go too far away. Razor has dropped out of sight, and we're looking for him. If we need you, we will call."

"No problem. You know how to find me."

The officer left, and Jennifer closed the door behind him. The clock showed eight-fifteen, but she was in no hurry. She would have to be late getting to work. At least John should be happy to know that the *Gazette's* sensitive information was back in safe hands. She *hoped*.

Before putting on her jacket, she scrolled through the missed calls history on her cellphone. There would undoubtedly be some catching up to do with two days' worth of unanswered correspondence.

Eighteen different missed calls logged. No surprise there. But six of them were from her brother and two of the others from a number having her hometown area code and prefix. What could that mean?

"Hi, Sis," came her brother Jeremy's breathy voicemail message from early yesterday. "Please call me as soon as possible. It's urgent."

Her heart thumped. Such a message coming from Jeremy most likely meant trouble. Maybe with his wife or children. Or, with their father. Erwin Partridge was not old, but he was a heart patient, and hadn't been faring well since the death of his wife two years earlier. She scrolled again through the call log with a sinking feeling.

Mourners filed past Jennifer, Jeremy, and his wife Anne. Jennifer forced smiles and spoke kindly to relatives, friends, and acquaintances, brushing off inquiries about the bandage on her forehead. But inside she battled guilt. How could she have been so totally unreachable during the last hours of her father's life?

Erwin Partridge's memorial service had been brief and simple, officiated by Marvin Fiedler, the family's pastor. Partridge had bequeathed his body to medical science; there would be no burial ceremony until an unspecified later date.

The familiar sights and smells of the church's interior and furnishings felt oppressive, and she was eager to leave with Jeremy and Anne when their responsibilities had been concluded.

Her last time inside the building, other than for her mother's funeral, had been in the final weeks before she graduated high school, for a private conference with Pastor Fiedler in his church office—a meeting after which she had bolted from the church in tears and run home. An hour of awkward conversation with her parents afterward had not helped matters. Within a week she finalized her plans to move to Minneapolis right after graduation, enroll at the University, and forge a new life—far away from Cedarfield.

Eventually, the last few attendees slipped out of the church. Jennifer and Jeremy moved about the sanctuary, picking up extra bulletins and collecting the guest book and a large basket overflowing with sympathy cards.

Pastor Fiedler approached. "Sorry for your loss, Jennifer. Your parents were very dear to me and to our church."

"Thank you, Pastor." Ugh! *Pastor.* What a distasteful label. She looked around for Jeremy, hoping her brother would suddenly appear to rescue her from this awkward situation. But he and Anne had gone into the adjoining fellowship hall. She moved quickly to join them.

Fiedler followed her to where Jeremy was helping himself to sandwiches left over from the reception. Jennifer poured herself a glass of water and went over to where Anne sat.

"Take all the time you need." Fiedler said. "The ladies will clean everything up. Please lock the door behind you if you are the last ones out."

He left, and the three Partridges sat.

Jeremy broke the silence. "Dad left you in charge of everything, Sis."

"How well I know. But I have my career. Responsibilities. I don't *want* to take time off. I have no interest whatsoever in spending time back here and dealing with this community. You, Jeremy, of all people should understand that."

"Well, Anne and I aren't competing with you for the honor. We've got two children and one more on the way."

Anne patted her belly. "Yes, I'm due in a little over a month."

"And we live over fifty miles away." Jeremy continued his litany of excuses. "My job keeps me tied down. And, financially speaking, I can't afford to take any more time off. I've even used vacation time this past week. But it's a moot point anyway; you're on the paper-work. You're the one that Dad trusted."

"Yeah… I know," Jennifer sighed. "It's too much to think about. He passed away so suddenly. Then there's the house. It's full of stuff and will need work before we can put it on the market. I wish he would have sold it after Mom died. That would have made things so much easier."

Even as she reasoned with her brother, a haunting, persistent notion had taken up residence in her thoughts. One which wouldn't go away, despite her efforts to suppress it. One which she was not about to confess to her brother or to anyone else.

Three days earlier, she had listened to the two remaining voice messages on her phone. Both had been placed by Mr. Swenson, the long-time owner and publisher of Cedarfield's own weekly news-paper, the *Cedarfield Voice*. The paper needed a full-time reporter and feature writer, and her name had come up repeatedly as the best candidate for the position.

This afternoon, Mr. Swenson had approached her following the memorial service, offered his condolences, and then compelled her to contact him before she left town.

But accepting his job offer meant giving up on her dreams and moving back to Cedarfield. No way that was happening! She be-longed in Minneapolis, delighted with and thriving in her position with the *Gazette*. A good income, an active social life, and a fine apartment in the trendy Uptown district. She was not about to let go of that to move back to a place that she had abandoned after gradu-ating high school. Her dad was gone; there was no reason to move back to Cedarfield. That was simply not an option. It *couldn't* be.

Or could it?

A robin flitted back and forth, gathering small twigs for his nest in the maple tree which Jennifer and her dad had planted on her tenth birthday. She watched his actions absently while curling her toes in the cool green grass in the back yard of her childhood home. The warm Saturday afternoon sun beaming down upon the lawn brought the pleasant scent of earth and new plant growth to her nostrils, temporarily lulling her mind into a state of reminiscing about the simpler days of her childhood, when the advent of spring meant that she and her friends could finally get outdoors. For space and privacy, away from Jeremy and his annoying friends and their video games. And from her uncles, who spent way too much time with her dad in the garage or the family room.

Those years gave way to junior high, and then to high school, where her science teacher encouraged her to challenge the faith of her childhood, even to the point of questioning the existence of God and the biblical account of Creation. Her history teacher deplored religious idealism as the basis for most if not all the world's major conflicts and wars. Jennifer had become intrigued with new perspectives of looking at the world and matters of faith and was not hesitant to air her thoughts and questions

By her senior year she and Kevin, Pastor Fiedler's nephew, had been dating seriously for several months, even entertaining notions of marriage and a future together in their hometown—until the afternoon that she met with Fiedler at his church office to ask what she believed to be innocent and reasonable questions about matters of faith and what she had been hearing in school.

But instead of engaging in what she hoped would be a healthy dialogue, the pastor appeared unprepared for her questions. He became angry and declared that her inflammatory notions had put her on a dangerous path, and that she was not suitable for any serious relationship with his nephew.

Soon after that Kevin broke things off. Jennifer left Cedarfield after graduation, never looking back.

Now she sat, frustrated and indignant over having been thrust back into this world by circumstances beyond her control.

At least today would be a break from the routine of the more than two weeks since her father's passing. Especially, the past two days. Thursday, a marathon of meetings. First with their attorney, then at the bank, then an auction house, and later with a realtor. Then several more hours spent with Jeremy in the house's attic, basement, and garage, poring through their father's personal belongings, an emotionally exhausting effort.

Then there had been Friday's meeting with Mr. Swenson at the *Voice*. Why had she agreed to meet with him? Somehow, his job offer had piqued her interest.

Someone behind honked, and Jennifer looked up. The traffic light had turned green.

"Sorry." She formed the word on her lips. Her car was southbound on Lyndale Avenue, but her mind was far away, locked in a struggle between defiance and surrender. No one was going to tell her what to do with her life.

Still...a persistent, unsettling feeling. Not only was her resolve being challenged; right now she didn't feel safe—a fleeting yet disturbing sensation. Was she at risk in some way, even this morning? Razor had not bothered her since the night of her fateful encounter, but that didn't mean that he couldn't... or wouldn't.

No! Fear would not win, and other people's opinions did not count. She would pursue and protect her vision; embrace her chosen career and personal life. It was, after all, her choice. Her own free will.

She parked next to the *Gazette* building, steeling herself to face whatever John had in store for the meeting he had called this morning. But with her car door open and one foot on the ground, Jennifer froze. Across the wide boulevard to her left, a tall and slender man was leaning against the side of a parked vehicle, watching her.

Razor?

At this distance she couldn't be certain, but she didn't want whoever it was to think that she was watching him. She grabbed her pack and marched into the building without looking back.

Heart thumping, she willed herself to refocus; John was waiting. Today, another Monday morning in the familiar environs; the building itself; the sights and sounds of the business activities coming to life for the day; the friendly nods and waves of co-workers in the hallway or from cubicles and doorways. Were their friendly waves those of greeting? Or of fond farewells?

Finally, her own office. Her space and its furnishings hadn't changed, but somehow appeared foreign, as if she no longer belonged, instead looking in from outside, as through a window or a camera lens. Something was gone.

What was that expression on John's face? She tapped politely on the doorframe and shuffled into his office for the appointed meeting. He looked thoughtful, concerned.

"How was your time in Cedarfield last week?" It was not a casual inquiry.

"Fine. About what I expected. A few meetings and a lot of sorting through my dad's papers, all part of trying to settle an estate. But I suspect that you didn't call me in this morning to ask about my weekend."

John looked at her with a blank expression, which she found unnerving. Maybe he's trying to figure out who he's going to hire to replace me. Or if he needs to repaint my office when I'm gone.

"Have you heard any more from the police?" His question betrayed his lingering concern over the authorities' yet unsuccessful search for Razor.

"Officer Burns has called me a couple of times. Unfortunately, the police have no new developments." There was no need to mention the man she had just seen outside; he may or may not have been Razor.

"Let's talk about what I called you in for this morning."

"Sure."

"Jen, your issue puzzles me," he said at last.

"What's so puzzling about it?"—The nerve of the man! — "I've explained my dilemma. The tug-of-war between my life and career here and my new responsibilities at home. Not to mention Mr. Swenson's relentless insistence that I come and work for him at the *Voice*. The guy doesn't give up."

"So, what's the problem? Make a decision and live with the consequences. That's what you tell me all the time."

"Yes, but I have responsibilities in both places. To you here, and to the situation in Cedarfield. Personal responsibilities, not even considering the newspaper job there."

"So… you're torn, you say. You're wrestling within yourself with this decision."

Jennifer grew more irritated. John was her boss, not a shrink. "Yes."

"Then what do you want?"

"I love my job here. And my life here. I want to stay."

"Then stay and keep working for the *Gazette*. You are a great asset to me and to the paper. In fact, I'll give you all the time off that you need to finish up your business back in Cedarfield. No deadline. No pressure." He shrugged, still without expression. "This is what you want. Just do it."

"It's not that simple. I'm the legal executor of the estate, with little help from my brother. My responsibilities will keep me away far longer than I could ever ask of you."

"Not a problem. Like I told you, take all the time you need." John raised his eyebrows. "But that's not the issue for you, is it."

"Hmph!"

"If you don't mind my saying so, it sounds like, at this juncture, things boil down to more than your taking care of your father's affairs. I believe you're in the throes of a bigger dilemma. Maybe even wrestling with your conscience, your inner voice."

"Sure, I do care about all of that. But that's not what you call a conscience. I'm simply looking at my options and trying to make the most practical decision."

"I understand. You want to do the right thing… oh, yeah… whatever 'right' means."

Something shifted inside of Jennifer. "I mean, do what's best in this particular situation. Simple. No need for you to psychoanalyze me."

"Psychoanalyze you? Not hardly. But the fact that you are weighing this decision speaks volumes to me." John became more animated. "The Jennifer Partridge that I've known for the time you've worked here didn't struggle in the way that you have this time."

"So, you say," she replied, her resolve slipping away.

"And there's this." John leaned back in his chair, staring upward as if the script for his next statement was etched into the ceiling. "Let's step back and look at a whole different angle to your situation. We'll begin with the absurd notion that maybe it's not all about what *you* think you want and how *you* feel about everything."

"For instance…?"

"Let's go back to what happened on that fateful night nearly a month ago. Hasn't it occurred to you how odd it was that a thug like Razor dumped you off relatively unharmed after drugging and abducting you, and that you got all your belongings returned to you intact? And you tell me you've not been bothered by Razor or any of his crowd since then, have you?"

Jennifer shook her head without comment, not liking where the conversation was going.

John continued. "Things could have turned out differently. You could have wound up getting beaten, raped, or even shot. And losing all your stuff—phone, laptop, wallet, and company files. What would your brother have done if he couldn't have gotten in touch with you? Explain that with your pat logic of 'actions and consequences.' Explain to me how you can even imagine that you have been in charge of your circumstances in all of this."

"That is what happened. Don't be throwing your 'what-ifs' at me. Don't go reading anything into it."

John continued, undeterred. "Then there's the matter of Mr. Swenson. Have you ever considered the possibility that the man knows something that you don't? Maybe that you're *supposed* to accept that position with his paper?"

"No way! That's my decision to make. Not his or anyone else's."

"I'll be straight with you, Jen. I would hate to lose you as an employee. But I can't stop you either if it's not meant to be. Who knows? The position with the *Cedarfield Voice* could turn out to be your dream job. Even more so than this one. You may be meant to return to your home in Cedarfield, to become a lifelong resident. You may grow to love it there."

An abhorrent notion! "Not hardly. That'll never happen."

"Are you sure? Are you in charge here?"

"Yes. In charge of myself. Of my decisions."

But Jennifer's throat had tightened, and her last words came out strained. She slouched in her chair. "Now I'm feeling tired and confused. Way too much to think about on a Monday morning."

John rubbed the stubble of his beard. "I'll sum it up this way. What happened to you the other night might be considered a divine appointment. You may be on the verge of an epiphany—if you would acknowledge it."

"A divine appointment? An epiphany?"

John sighed, for the first time betraying impatience. "Open your eyes, Jen. Take a deep breath and look at what's going on here. Be honest with yourself. I believe that this whole situation is bigger than you. Sometimes, you can't ignore what's obvious. And, whether you like it or not, you may already have your answer. Just let go."

Matthew 5:3 (KJV)
Blessed are the poor in spirit: for theirs is the kingdom of heaven.

Matthew 5:3 (AMP)
Blessed [spiritually prosperous, happy, to be admired] are the poor in spirit [those devoid of spiritual arrogance, those who regard themselves as insignificant], for theirs is the kingdom of heaven [both now and forever].

Matthew 5:3 (MSG)
You're blessed when you're at the end of your rope. With less of you there is more of God and his rule.

TODD

The phone on Todd Peterson's desk buzzed. "There's a Mr. Dierks here at the front desk. He says he needs to see you."

"Tanya, I'm not sure that I know a 'Mr. Dierks.' Get his first name please."

A long pause, with muffled conversation. "Zachary Dierks. Says he has a delivery for you."

Zach? No! Not here! He cradled the phone, raised halfway up out of his chair, leaned to his right, and looked out through his office doorway to the reception area, some forty feet away. A tall, lean man with charcoal-colored hair and a thin moustache and dressed in a gray pinstriped suit, was seated in the reception area, the familiar-looking briefcase at his feet. That was Zach, a dangerous man. A predator. A man who had no business being here.

This was Todd's turf, his eighth-floor corner office with a breathtaking view of downtown Minneapolis and St. Anthony Falls. Challenging and satisfying work, and coworkers that he enjoyed. Off-limits to Zachary Dierks.

The unwelcome guest looked relaxed enough, stretched out comfortably in a leather chair. Narrow eyes shifting back and forth, taking in every detail of the reception area as would a hunter surveying the habitat of his prey. Fine mahogany furniture; the brass-colored company logo on the wall over Tanya's desk; the young and attractive receptionist herself; the folded copy of the *Wall Street Journal* on the table next to his chair; the expensively dressed man and woman who walked by.

That was Zach all right. Along with showing up where he didn't belong to intimidate, he would be on the lookout for potential new customers. The man had a nose for money and an instinct for opportunity, and would be fairly drooling in this environment, which attracted wealthy investors and other clientele having an abundance of resources. Characteristically, he had dressed for the part. Todd recognized the tailored, thousand-dollar suit; he owned one like it himself.

He'd have to deal with the snake, and then get rid of him.

"Good morning, Zach. How nice to see you."

"Hi Todd. My pleasure." He stood and threw a disarming smile at Tanya. "Thank you, sweetheart."

Todd stepped in front of her, deliberately turning his back toward Zach, blocking his view. "Mr. Dierks and I will be in my office for a few minutes. Please hold any calls."

"Sure thing." Oblivious to his agitated state, she turned her attention back to the stack of unopened mail on her desk.

Seething, he led the way back to his office, ushered Zach inside, and pressed the door shut behind them.

"I've told you to never come to my workplace! Never!"

"Yes, so you've told me." Dierks calmly ambled about, eyes up and down, attending to every detail of the small room, even picking up a crystal sculpture from a side table and lobbing it back and forth in his hands.

"Then what's going on? Why are you here?" Todd's eyes followed the arc of the moving piece, an expensive gift from one of his clients.

Zach said nothing but gently set it down. Then lifted his briefcase, placed it on top of the desk, and flipped it open. Inside were what Todd had suspected and feared. Neat rows of plastic packets.

8 balls of cocaine. By his own quick estimation, probably ten to twelve thousand dollars' worth.

"As if you don't know. Don't mess with me, Peterson. I've come to collect what's due, and to drop off some more of my wares. Who knows? Maybe one or two of your co-workers would like to join us in our little enterprise."

Repulsed at the notion, Todd involuntarily turned around to scan the outside wall of glass behind his desk.

"Chill out, man," Zach sneered. "No one's looking over your shoulder way up here."

"Clever." He turned back, reached out, and slammed the case shut before dropping into his chair. "I've asked you to never ever show up here, much less bring that stuff in here." He cast a wary glance toward the long vertical window in his office door.

"Too bad." Zach leaned over, planting both palms on the desktop. "I've asked you all week for my money. The way I see it, you owe me about ten grand. I'm tired of waiting."

"Hey, I promised to bring it to you, and I will. You don't understand my world."

"Your world *is* my world, Peterson."

"No, it's not! You are a small part of my world, the part that begins *after* my daytime working hours, outside of this building, and subject to my personal schedule. Don't try to bully me."

"That's fine. But I still expect to get paid on time."

"Sure, you do. You want everything your way and on your terms." He rose and jabbed a finger toward Zach's chest. "You enjoy the benefits of partnering with me, given my day job. The circles I move in and the caliber of clients within my reach. But that comes at a cost to both of us. Twelve-hour workdays this week, and out of town for two of those days. There are simply not enough hours in the week. But don't worry, I have your money… but not here, obviously."

"Then where? You don't like having me show up at your work, and maybe soliciting your co-workers? Then, at least keep me informed."

"Okay, fine." Aware of the volume of their voices, Todd looked toward the door. Still no sign of anyone else nearby. He would have to wrap this up.

Zach picked up his briefcase. "You get mercy this time, Mr. Peterson. Name a time and place. I'll walk out of here all nice and polite, but you've got to work with me according to our agreement."

"Fair enough. Then I'll settle with you tonight, at our usual spot. What time?"

"Ten o'clock. And, by the way, I am glad to finally see where you spend your days. Pretty snazzy setup you got here. It smells like opportunity. Money, and future customers—and maybe even a fun night out with your hot-looking receptionist."

"Don't even think about it."

"Remember. Ten o'clock. And bring the cash." He turned, pulled open the door, and strutted out, flashing a wide smile at Tanya on his way past her desk.

Todd pulled a handkerchief from his pocket and wiped his face. He had dealt with Zach for nearly two years and always knew that he could not be trusted. But the man had never before showed up at his office. Even worse was the fact that he had brought a stash with him. It seemed that the Zach's notion of boundaries had slipped. He would have to rein the guy in.

Todd nursed his third beer, barely tasting the drink which had warmed to room temperature. Already ten-thirty and still no sign of Zach. He was not surprised; the man habitually ran late, his way of flexing his power and authority. Nevertheless, he had made it a point to be on time himself; where his shadowy partner had today made the unprecedented move of showing up unannounced at Harkin Financial's offices, he would take extra measures to be sure that didn't happen again.

Inside his jacket, folded up on the seat beside him, were two thick envelopes containing a total of almost ten thousand dollars in hundreds and twenties, the proceeds of nearly two weeks of sales, less his own cut.

Despite the cool temperatures in the place, his forehead was coated with a thin layer of perspiration, and he unbuttoned and tugged at his collar to loosen it. An ultimatum was in order; this business had to end. The money wasn't that important, not worth the stress. In truth, he didn't even need the cocaine, merely an occasional recreational indulgence with added benefit of providing spending money. Nothing further.

Their habitual meeting spot in a corner booth in Schlampy's afforded an unobstructed view of not only the front entryway, but of the length and breadth of the room and the doorways leading to the rest rooms and kitchen at the rear. At this hour on a Friday evening, the place was filled with customers. Most of the booths and tables were occupied, and servers hustled about with platters of burgers, sandwiches, and salads.

Zach, Todd knew, was tight with the owners of the establishment and would be making his entrance from the rear, having entered the building from the alley and making his usual "inspection" pass through the kitchen. That was the man's Achilles' heel, he had realized; the otherwise cunning and wary thug was an incurable creature of habit. Predicable to the point of putting himself in peril at times.

Sure enough. Ten minutes later the familiar tall figure stepped through the kitchen door, pinstriped suit, briefcase, and all. Without breaking stride, he signaled a short, stout woman behind the bar— "Bring me the usual, Honey" —and approached the booth, sliding into the seat, face dark and jaw set. "Got my money?"

"All right here." After quick glance about for any curious on-lookers, Todd pulled both envelopes from his jacket and slid them across the table, where Zach whisked them out of view.

Todd took the offensive. "You know, I don't need this gig anymore."

"No, Peterson. I get it that you don't need the money. As of this morning, I've even gotten to see that posh office that you enjoy downtown. You're a high roller. A big shot in the world of commercial real estate. Yep, you probably don't need my money."

"Then you understand that I may want out of this."

Zach paused as the waitress set a tall glass of beer before him and walked away.

"You '*may* want out of this', you say. Boy, that sounded decisive!" He smirked. "You say that, but I know better. Because, while you don't need the money—and while, admittedly, you don't particularly care for me—you do need this." He tapped the briefcase. "You see, it's obvious that you are one of your own best customers. A portion of this bundle of money that you've handed me is your own, correct?"

"Maybe," Todd muttered, grimly realizing that his partner had taken control of the conversation.

"Don't 'maybe' me! You enjoy your fix as much as most of your customers do. That's what helps you perform so well at work and put in those long days that you've whined about. I've been in this busi-ness long enough to be able to read my customers, and my partners. Face it, buddy, you're in. Whether you like it or not."

"But that's my own business. My choice. What's it to you if I indulge or not?"

"Frankly, I don't care whether you use or not. But here's why I'm not letting you off the hook. You happen to be one of my best partners. Face it, Peterson. You're good at what you do, good for my business."

"Don't try to flatter me."

"Flatter you? Not hardly. It's no secret that you mingle with the crowd that can best afford what we provide. While most of my boys are hanging out in the parks and on the street corners and in dumps like this, you spend your evenings in the high-end clubs downtown and the five-star hotels out on the strip."

"Once again, in the end it's still my choice. My decision."

"Maybe so, but here's your problem. You're a businessman, smart enough to understand that your commission income from me far exceeds what you spend for what little you use. And I provide the best stuff. I'd like to see you try to find something as pure as my supply anywhere else around here."

"You're a manipulative jerk. You can't use me this way."

"Use you?" Zach sat back and laughed at the ceiling. "Remember what you told me. Your choice, my friend. Sure. Go your own way. But you'll be back. I know you."

The crack of the bat, and the ball arced over the head of the second baseman and dropped into center field, well out of reach of the outfielder who scrambled to retrieve it. Trevor had gotten a hit and driven in a run.

"That's my boy!" Kyle Tomlinson hopped up and raised a fist on an outstretched arm. "See. I told you he'd get a hit. He knows how to keep his eye on the ball. He can connect with a pitch more consistently than most kids his age."

"I'm impressed. Your hours of working with him have paid off."

Todd and Kyle were the sole occupants of the top row of bleachers set behind home plate in a city softball park. The 2001 season of summer leagues was underway, and Todd's attendance at the weekend games of Kyle's son provided a convenient venue for combining business with pleasure. He enjoyed the occasional break from his usual environs of hotel lounges and night clubs; Kyle celebrated the success of his son. And he and Kyle were able to conduct what had become a routine transaction without drawing anyone's attention.

"Hey, I'm starving. Let's eat," Todd said, according to script.

While all eyes of the small crowd were focused on the playing field, he had handed Kyle a soft drink and a small white paper bag displaying a local fast food restaurant logo and containing a double-hamburger and fries—along with additional contents.

Kyle, in turn, reached into his pocket and handed back a wad of several bills. "Here, keep the change." No one would suspect that the denominations of those bills were not ones, but twenties and hundreds.

The two men had known each other for over a year. Kyle, a personal investment advisor, had introduced himself to Todd at a conference. The two became regular happy-hour friends, and Todd soon discerned Kyle's mild cocaine habit. He became supplier of his needs, offering a reduced price for the goods. In turn, Kyle managed a small personal investment account for Todd. Thus began a cordial business relationship that had evolved into a friendship.

But tonight, Kyle's reaction upon receiving his supply was different. Instead of opening the bag, he set it down between his feet, waiting for several minutes before finally poking his hand in and pulling out his wrapped hamburger. Almost as if he were afraid of touching it.

In front of them a batter struck out, ending the inning and leaving Trevor stranded on first base. Kyle turned his attention away from the game and looked at Todd, then lowered his head. "I've got a problem."

"Oh? Money?"

"No, it's not that. But I've had a couple of screwups, including two days of missed work. Both my wife and my boss are starting to ask questions. It's not just this stuff" —he pointed to the bag— "but my drinking, too."

"Ooh, that's not good."

"Right. Frankly, I'm afraid of losing it. This has been a great year for me so far, financially speaking. I can't afford to blow it—through a straw or any other way."

"I understand. If you were to lose your job, your income…"

"Yes, but it's more than that. It's my conscience. I can't keep on this way, you know, hiding everything. The hypocrisy and guilt. The whole racket."

"You know I'm not demanding anything of you." Todd reached into his pocket. "Here, I'll return your money if you want."

"No. I asked you to bring it, and a deal's a deal. But this may be the end of it for me."

"Whatever you say. No pressure from me."

"Thanks. But I'm telling you, I'm afraid of where this is going for me. I've decided to come clean with my wife and my boss and get myself under control."

"Do whatever you think best." He placed his hand on Kyle's shoulder. "But please keep my name out of it."

"Understood. I consider you a friend, not merely a business partner. I'll protect you."

"Thanks. Glad to hear that. Whatever you decide to do, I'd like to keep the relationship. And my investment account. And I'll even keep coming out to watch Trevor play ball."

"Mighty generous of you. I hope that my bailing out doesn't create issues for you. This is messy business, especially in your position. I know you answer to others."

"Oh, Kyle, don't worry about me. I've got it all under control."

Four more innings and the game ended. Trevor's team had lost, but the game had been a personal victory for Trevor, his having driven in a run and later scored himself.

Todd watched Kyle and Trevor walk toward their car together, Kyle's right arm around his son's shoulders and his left arm pressed against the side pocket of his jacket which contained the tightly folded food sack and its contents.

He walked back to his own car, pondering his friend's circumstance and pending decisions. Kyle was a husband and a father. A man who could not afford to compromise his functioning, especially to the point of losing his job. Wasn't that what often happened with addicts and alcoholics? Their work performance lagged, and they got fired. Then they wound up in rehab somewhere. Then divorced. If rehab didn't work, then they wound up on the street. Or dead.

But not Todd Peterson. He managed things well. A generous salary and commission arrangement in his profession, and job security with the same firm for more than five years. And he had no wife or children to support or answer to. While he might lose Kyle's business, there were others. He still enjoyed a lucrative trade with a short list of customers who were willing to routinely shell out cash for their supply, an income which far exceeded the expense of his own small habit.

But something nagged at him. Kyle and Trevor were on their way home to wife and mother. What kind of woman was Mrs. Tomlinson? Her temperament, her strength, her reaction. How would she handle the news that her husband had an alcohol and drug habit, possibly an addiction? What would happen then?

Kyle had never described his wife's appearance, but Todd, closing his eyes, could see her, almost as vividly as looking at a color photograph. A pretty woman with shoulder-length brunette hair and deep brown eyes. A strong woman, one who could handle her husband's situation, set him back on the right path.

He didn't understand what had just transpired in his thoughts, but he suddenly felt a measure of relief for his friend. Kyle had married the right woman. She would help him do the right thing. He would be okay after all.

His phone buzzed. Carly. Not what he needed.

"Hi." He answered without enthusiasm. Carly, a graphic artist and one of his regular after-hours customers, had also become his off-and-on partner in a relationship, a relationship he was ready to be done with, due to her escalating cocaine use and abuse of prescribed antidepressants. He regretted answering the call, even before he heard her voice.

"Hey, baby," she cooed. "What're you doing?"

"I've been with my friend Kyle at the ball field. We watched his kid play."

"Oh, how sweet of you. Would you like to come over tonight? Ravioli on the menu. Made the pasta myself from scratch, my grandmother's recipe. And a bottle of wine. I don't want to eat alone."

"Oh, thank you for asking, but I can't. I promised Kyle that I'd go over to his place for dinner tonight." The lie flowed easily from his lips.

"Todd, honey. What about me? You and I used to spend all of our Sunday evenings together."

"Yes, but not this time I'm afraid."

The line went dead. Predictably, she was upset and pouting. He shrugged and dropped the phone back into his pocket. He had enough to deal with; putting up with Carly was not on the list.

"Why is Del calling for a meeting this morning? At nine o'clock? That's a half-hour from now." Todd's voice carried all the way from his office to the reception area.

"Good morning! Nice to see you too," Tanya sang out, leaning around in her chair to cast him an exaggerated smile.

"Thanks for the sarcasm. But I've just rolled in. I've been blindsided." He stormed up to the front desk, having scanned the usual deluge of Monday morning emails, his attention immediately drawn to the one from Delbert Harkin.

"Hey, chill! You're scaring me." Her face betrayed fright at his uncharacteristically aggressive approach.

He planted both hands on her desk and leaned forward to view her screen. "The email. Didn't you read the email?"

"What email are you talking about?" She said. "Are you okay?"

"The one about the meeting. The *urgent* meeting. In Del's office." He stabbed a finger toward the wall clock. "In less than thirty minutes."

"Nope." She scanned her screen. "No such email invitation for me. Must have gone to you alone. Hmm… a *private, urgent* meeting. Aren't you special!"

"Whew!" He paced about the small reception area, clenching and unclenching both hands. "Del never—I mean *never*—calls me in on short notice like this. And what does urgent mean?"

"What's going on? Why so hyper? It's a meeting."

Without responding, he turned and walked back to his own office, closed the door, and fell into his chair. His mistake, he realized, was snorting this morning, in the parking lot before coming into the building, thereby breaking his own rules. Now he was agitated, fidgety, paranoid. He had only a few minutes to get a hold of himself.

In the privacy of his office, his imagination slipped into high gear. Whether it was from the effects of the drug or not, it felt very real. He was mentally transported from the office back to his own home, where he watched Harkin force open his front door and enter, bent on searching through his personal belongings, desk drawers, refrigerator, medicine cabinet. Searching…

He leaned back and closed his eyes. Eventually, the sensation subsided, and he opened his eyes. Five minutes to go. Enough time to get to the men's room and splash some cold water on his face before going to his meeting.

The placard on the door read Delbert J. Harkin, President. Todd tapped lightly.

"Come in." The distinguished founder of Harkin Financial looked grim. "Sit down please."

He sat.

"Peterson, I'm worried about you."

"Worried? How so?" He clutched his hands in his lap so that Harkin wouldn't see the trembling.

"Don't get me wrong. You are one of our top representatives here. Your work has been stellar for the past five years. And that's what concerns me."

"I don't understand. Is something wrong?"

"I pay attention to small things. Details. Including small changes in my employees' habits, performance, behaviors, and so forth. And that's why I've called you in this morning."

"Sir, you'll have to be more specific. Something with me?"

"Yes, unfortunately. Last week you slipped up. Twice. Most uncharacteristic for you."

"Slipped up?" Todd wilted. "How? When?"

"Friday. You missed the dinner meeting altogether."

"Oh… that was Friday, wasn't it."

"Yes, it was. Charles Abernathy and I waited at the Beaumont Club for over an hour, wondering where you were and why you wouldn't answer your phone. I wound up finalizing the deal myself."

"Ooh, gosh, I'm sorry." He pulled out his pocket calendar. "You're right. I had it scheduled. I just missed it. Brain freeze I guess."

"Granted, it can happen. We all forget at times. But there were also mistakes on the Weatherly contract, the one you handed to me—also on Friday."

"Mistakes? Where?"

Harkin stepped over to his desk and picked up a folder, which he handed to Todd. "Let's see if you can find them."

He scanned the three-page contract. Oh, no! The name of one of Weatherly's competitors appeared in three different places on the form.

"I can't believe I did that." He raked his hands through his hair, fighting a sense of alarm. "But I see how it happened. I used another contract as a template—you know, saving it under a new file name. We do it all the time. In this case I forgot to change the client name in all the places."

"Fortunately for us, I caught the mistakes before I signed it and had it delivered." Harkin said nothing further, but the expression on his face spoke volumes.

"I am so sorry, sir. I don't know what else to say."

"Todd." He leaned forward and spoke in a fatherly tone. "I'm not angry. I'm puzzled. How did this happen with you? Your work has been accurate and consistent for years. You rarely make a mistake, and you never miss an appointment. What's happened?"

Todd groaned within. He knew exactly what had happened on Friday: Zach's unexpected appearance in the office that morning, impairing his concentration for the rest of the day. But for Harkin's alertness, a long-standing client relationship could have been jeopardized.

But, more concerning, he was forced to confront his own vulnerability. Maybe his other activities were interfering with his work performance after all.

"This will never happen again. I promise."

Harkin reached over and clasped his hand. "I hope not. If you're in trouble, or if you need help in any way, I'm here for you. But I need to see the caliber of work that you've always maintained. Your job here depends on it. Our company is counting on you."

"Yes, sir." He stood and scrambled to the door. He couldn't wait for this day to be over, and to get home—to privacy, and to where he could self-medicate.

A week passed. Then two. Seemingly, the longest weeks of his life. By day, plying his profession under the watchful eye of at least Harkin, if not everyone else. Had everyone in the office become aware of his issues?

During workdays, he steeled himself against the persistent temptation to step out to his car for a fix, double-checked all his work, and avoided any unnecessary client meetings or other social engagements. Most of his days were spent sequestered in his office. Harkin, he knew, was watching.

Evenings and Saturdays were spent in the Twin Cities' finer night clubs and hotel lounges, conducting trade with the small circle of his regular customers. With Zach hounding him, there was no choice.

Then there was Carly. He somehow didn't have the backbone to put an end to that toxic relationship, which was sinking to new lows due to her ever increasing demands for both his time and his wares.

At least he had kept up his payment arrangements to Zach's satisfaction. The man had not made any more visits to his office, instead being content to conduct all business at Schlampy's.

But Todd was wearing out. He didn't feel well anymore and had lost weight. His co-workers were bound to notice, and it was only a matter of time before the thin thread of his existence would snap.

One bright spot: at least Kyle had stayed in touch by phone. His faithful friend had taken the giant step; he still had his wife, still had his son, and still had his job. He was currently enrolled in an accountability program which included weekly counseling sessions. It would be a long and difficult journey for Kyle, but he was off to a good start.

So, what was he himself to do? Something had to give.

Steady rains pelted the window, and branches from a large maple tree scraped against the front of the house in high winds. Todd lay wide awake, listening to the sounds of the blustery Saturday morning outside. His body seemed unwilling to move. At least there were no responsibilities today.

This might be a day to relax at home and watch golf on television, a welcomed time of relief after what may have been one of the most stressful weeks of his life. Calling in sick on Monday. Coming into work on Tuesday and somehow closing three client deals without any mistakes, a seeming miracle. Walking on eggshells for the remainder of the week, aware that Harkin was going behind him, double-checking his work. Mercifully, the man had not called him back into his office. No more questions… at least for now.

Added to that, a contentious meeting with Zach on Tuesday evening. Supply had become plentiful, and the guy was back to bullying. More customers were needed and any efforts at setting limits seemed in vain.

Finally, his own habit, which had ramped up along with his load of stress, last night being the most recent occurrence. If this coming week didn't go better than last week had, he'd truly be in trouble. His job was no longer a certainty. For that matter, his whole life and well-being was no longer a certainty. Not while he was a slave to the cocaine, to his handful of customers, and to Zach. He pulled the covers up over his face. It was all too much. Something had to give.

A pounding on the front door forced him out of bed.

What gives? Who would be at his door this time of day on a crummy, rainy Saturday?

He stumbled toward the closet and pulled on a pair of jeans and a T-shirt. "Hold on! I'm coming!" More pounding. He lurched barefooted into the front hallway and swung open the door.

Zach!

"What're you doing here?" He spit out angry words. Zach had never before come to his home. He suddenly felt vulnerable, frightened. First his place of work, and now his home. Were there no boundaries with this guy?

"Hello friend. I came by to thank you for paying your debts on time." With rain dripping from his hooded jacket, he chirped away, ignoring Todd's grogginess. "May I come in?"

"I suppose so." Do I have any choice?

He stepped into the foyer and unzipped his jacket, sprinkling droplets of water across the floor. "Thank you for inviting me in, Peterson."

"How could I refuse? Make yourself at home."

"Hey, cut the sarcasm." Zach pulled a slip of paper from his shirt pocket. "I've got a couple more customers for you. A man and a woman. Professionals, both of them. High rollers. Your caliber."

"Oh, great."

"Hey, what's your problem? I stuck my neck out to land these guys. You okay?"

"Still out of it. You woke me out of a sound sleep."

"Well, Peterson, you'd better wake up. Duty calls. You're the guy to deal with these types. So, follow up with them. You make that happen, or I might show up here, or at your office again. Do you want that?"

"No. Like I've told you, I'm maxed out between holding my day job together plus handling your business. No more! I'm even thinking of getting out altogether. The last thing I want is more customers. You can keep them for yourself."

"Don't talk to me that way. I tend to be sensitive and vindictive. If I can't persuade you myself through polite conversation, being the gentleman that I am, then maybe one of my partners can motivate you."

"Your partners? You've never mentioned any partners before."

"Peterson, you don't think I operate alone, do you? You and I, we're part of something bigger. Yessiree, there are others around here that know how well you perform, and who will notice if you choose not to do so. But I warn you, they're not merciful like I am. In fact, I've got one of them with me here this morning."

"With you? Where?"

"Right here." Zach flipped open the flap of his rain jacket and pulled out a handgun, a shiny black .38 caliber from a shoulder holster on his left side. He aimed it at Todd's chest. "Do you understand? If you quit working with me, that's the same as taking money out of my pocket. Do you think I'm going to stand for that?"

A gun! This guy was nuts! Taking things to a whole new level! He had never looked down the barrel of a gun before. Any notion of challenging Zach's demands instantly disintegrated.

"I understand!" He snatched the slip of paper from Zach's other hand. "On second thought, I'd be more than happy to reach out to this couple."

"Okay, that's what I like to hear. Tell them I sent you." He holstered the gun, zipped up his jacket, and pulled the door open.

"Thank you for being so cooperative. I'm counting on you." He waved and left. Todd slammed the door. The interaction had lasted less than five minutes but left him quaking. This morning's encounter was not to drop off a message; it was to deliver a threat, and it was working.

Now fully awake, he moved into the kitchen and started the coffee maker, and then switched on the TV. The weather forecast for the day looked dismal. Cold and wind and rain. He would love to be able to crawl back into bed and hide under the covers or lose himself in watching some sporting event on television. But there would be no hiding out today. Zach was expecting action and would be following up before the weekend was out.

The aromas of brewed coffee and toast jogged his pattern of thought. He redirected his attention to fixing breakfast, recalling a recent conversation with Kyle, probably the only positive aspect of his current world. The man had come clean and seemed to be making it. Wow! The man was either courageous, or desperate, or both. But Kyle had a lot to lose. He was married and had children. He couldn't afford to fail.

But what about me? Todd sat on that thought while eating breakfast. Kyle couldn't afford to throw his life away, but neither could he himself. True, he wasn't married, had no kids. But he was young and still had a life and a future which may or may not include a spouse and family. A future that he didn't want to spend looking over his shoulder, catering to the whims of goons like Zach, or of needing a fix to function.

But whom could he talk with about his situation? The small circle of people who knew about his secret life were those with whom he dealt drugs, either as seller or buyer.

Refilling his coffee and carrying it over to his desk, he brought the PC screen to life and typed in keywords leading to a local drug addiction recovery hotline. Someone there could help. Maybe he could even find his way to some daylight before he had to deal with Zach any further.

He copied down a local contact number, but couldn't pick up his phone—not yet. Confession would be painful. And where would it lead? Would he then have to confess to Mr. Harkin? Would he lose his job after all? And how would he handle being cut off from being able to use? And give up drinking. Drug habits were serious, and breaking those habits was difficult. He had tried and failed once before. Was he up to this?

His phone buzzed where it lay on the desk. Zach! The jerk had just left and was calling again, way too soon. He let the call go to voicemail.

Todd then knew what he had to do. He picked up his phone and punched in the number to the hotline.

A calm female voice came on the line. "Hello. Thank you for calling. My name is Debbie."

"Uh, ah, hello." He had placed the call so impulsively that he hadn't had time to figure out what he was going to say. A long pause.

"Hello? May I help you?"

"Hi. Uh, yes, my name is Todd. I'm in a bad place this morning. In fact, I'm at the end of my rope. I might lose my job, I use cocaine, and I'm even afraid of getting hurt or killed."

"Well, Todd. You've done the right thing by calling. I'm here to help you. Please start at the beginning and tell me everything that is going on."

The phone call lasted nearly an hour. By the time he hung up, he had promised to pay an in-person visit to where he could get to help and safety. He clicked off the call, then pulled up the call log on his phone and deleted Zach's last voicemail without bothering to listen to it.

Today, I am going to get help. Zachary Dierks will have to wait, come what may.

Clutching his raincoat tightly against driving rain, Todd leaned into the wind and crossed the short distance from the parking lot to the door leading into a nondescript storefront along Lake Street, the counseling center.

"Is Debbie here?"

The petite, gray-haired woman at a desk inside nodded. "Sure. Your name please?"

"It's Todd. I spoke with her earlier this morning."

"Okay, Todd. Have a seat, and we'll be right with you."

He couldn't sit but paced about the waiting room. Front windows looked out upon the dreary morning, steady rains coming down onto a gray landscape of concrete, chain-link fences, and rows of one-story buildings. A dry-cleaner, a barber shop, an antique store, and a boarded-up service station. Worlds apart from his comfortable work environment two or three miles away in downtown Minneapolis.

Footsteps sounded, and a beaming face appeared in a doorway.

"Hello, Todd. I'm Debbie. Please come back here with me."

He looked up—and gave a start. This was Debbie? The crisis counselor? Precisely the same pretty face, the shoulder length brunette hair and brown eyes that he had envisioned as Kyle Tomlinson's wife a few weeks earlier! There was no mistake. It was the same person. He hadn't seen Kyle's wife after all! He had seen Debbie!

So… what did that mean?

Coming to his senses, he nodded politely to the woman behind the desk, and followed Debbie down a hall and through a doorway into a small room having a few pieces of furniture, a mini refrigerator, a coffee maker, and several large potted plants.

"Make yourself at home." She nodded toward a set of chairs on the left. "Coffee?"

"No, thank you. I've had plenty today." He sat, feeling more cheered in these warm surroundings.

"Before we go any further," Debbie began. "I need to once again ask you the number one most important question."

"Okay…?"

"Are you truly willing to go through with this? Whatever it takes?"

"That's why I'm here. Why would you ask me a question like that?"

"Oh, you'd be surprised at the number of those who come crawling to us for help, because they are in a bad spot or feeling overwhelmed emotionally or physically or financially. But then, after getting some of our attention, or get a measure of relief from their immediate pain… they quit."

"Okay. But not me. I'm going to see this through. My life depends on it."

"Please understand that I'm not trying to insult you, but I do need know that you're willing to work at this, to stay with me for the long haul. Make sense?"

"Yes, absolutely! I'm desperate. I have come to the end of myself, I promise."

"Then," she smiled again. "You're right where you need to be. Let's get started."

Fighting nausea and sitting on his trembling hands, Todd sat at his desk, looking over an array of contracts, comprehending nothing, but doing his best to look calm.

After having come clean a week earlier—first with Debbie, then with local law enforcement, and finally with Delbert Harkin himself—he was struggling with the initial throes of recovery, not only from his drug and alcohol habit, but from the abyss of pain, fear, and torment that his world had become.

It had been a grueling but productive week. With Debbie's counsel and advocacy, he had committed to a rehab regimen and negotiated a deal with the authorities through which he would help them break up a local drug ring in exchange for leniency in sentencing for his own activities.

Kyle would be proud. When this was all over, he would contact his friend.

Today—Monday—would likely be the culmination of everyone's collaborative efforts. All last week, he had purposely avoided meeting Zach, had ignored his calls, and had even left town for the weekend, knowing that he owed the man several thousand dollars. The snake, having failed to make contact elsewhere, would very likely show back up at Harkin Financial's offices this morning. But this time the outcome would be different.

He was not to be disappointed. Around eight-thirty Zach appeared at the front desk, attired in his tailored suit, and toting his briefcase. He greeted Tanya, while Todd discreetly observed him from his office—as did two other gentlemen, sitting in adjoining offices, appearing focused on their own computers. Plainclothes narcotics officers, dressed in fine business attire. If the thug happened to be carrying a supply of his wares to the office, the nightmare would be over in a matter of minutes. If he was packing his .38, so much the better.

Todd strode forward, heart pounding. "Good to see you again. Come on back."

Zach was not smiling. Without seeming to take notice of anyone else, he followed Todd back into his office, but then shut and locked the door himself before turning around, his face dark with anger.

"Peterson, you don't return my calls. You won't meet with me, and you weren't at home this weekend. And you owe me money.

I've about had it with you." He flipped open his suitcoat enough to reveal the butt of his holstered handgun.

Then he noticed Todd's drawn facial expression, trembling hands, and sweat-soaked shirt. His anger abated. "Man, you look washed out this morning. Long weekend? Maybe needing a fix, eh? I told you that you needed me. Or is my partner here scaring you?"

"Sorry. I've told you about how things go for me in this profession." He fought to remain calm while forming the rehearsed lie, his insides rolling in protest. "I happened to be out of town on business most of last week."

Offering no words of sympathy or understanding, Zach slapped the briefcase onto the desk and snapped open the lid. This time, rows of 8 balls along with several stacks of currency. "Look here, Peterson. I warned you. We're going to do business this morning. Right here and right now!"

"Yes, we are," he replied in a small voice, drawn between absolute terror and euphoria. Zach had taken the bait. All that remained was the prearranged signal to the waiting officers.

He went into his act, which didn't feel like acting at all. He looked at the stash, then suddenly bent over, clutching his stomach.

"What's the matter, my friend? Are you in desperate need of a fix? Or feeling sorry for failing me?"

Todd straightened up. "Probably all of the above. But my immediate problem takes priority. I'm about to toss my whole breakfast. I would highly recommend that you let me out of here to get to the bathroom."

Zach's face blanched. There was no time to think, to counter this abrupt maneuver. Involuntarily, he slammed the lid shut and stepped backward. Todd came around his desk, unlocked and flung open the door, and flew from the room and down a hallway in the direction of the men's room. He didn't want to be anywhere around when things went down.

Seconds later the two plainclothes officers moved from their respective positions and calmly walked toward where Zach—and his cocaine supply and his holstered gun—waited.

Matthew 5:4 (KJV)
Blessed are they that mourn: for they shall be comforted.

Matthew 5:4 (AMP)
Blessed [forgiven, refreshed by God's grace] are those who mourn [over their sins and repent], for they will be comforted [when the burden of sin is lifted].

Matthew 5:4 (MSG)
You're blessed when you feel you've lost what is most dear to you. Only then can you be embraced by the One most dear to you.

EZRA

The snap. Quarterback Davidson dropped back, looking to his left and to his right, shouting to his wide receivers. Waiting. Waiting.

Ezra Wilson shot forward on feet that seemed to glide over the turf. He ducked and twisted and side-stepped, sliding between two defensive backs as if they didn't exist. Then plunged ahead, a blur, easily weaving among two more defenders without a touch from either of them.

Davidson released the pass.

Wilson, crossing the opponents' thirty-yard line, pivoted to his left, one quick glance over his shoulder. Then twisted 180 degrees to the right and reached high, functioning more by sense than by sight, waiting. Attuned to the pounding and panting sounds of the cornerback close at hand, but oblivious to the roar of the crowd, on their feet as one.

Then the satisfying smack of the ball into both hands. He pulled it to his chest and darted forward, looking at a field completely open. Fourteen more yards and he trotted into the end zone. An easy touchdown.

"Man, you did it again!" Davidson clapped him on the back at the bench. "Danced your way right through their whole defensive secondary! The man who walks through walls."

"Hey, you put the ball right where it belonged. All I had to do was hang on to it."

As St. Paul Waukeshon High School's star wide receiver, Ezra Wilson held the acclaim of not only his teammates, but of the coaching staff, the student body, and the school's teachers and administration. In everyone's mind, he was destined for greater things in the world of college football, and the University of Minnesota was beckoning.

The kick following the touchdown was good and ensured a Waukeshon Tigers victory with seconds remaining in the game, thus sealing their place in their division's 1985 State Semifinals.

As the clock ran out, the mood at the bench was jubilant. Both Davidson and Wilson found themselves fending off the playful punches of their teammates. Coach Curt Hadoff pointed at Ezra. "Wilson, your performance tonight confirms that I know that I know. We're going to meet again. After the holiday break. I'll talk some sense into you yet."

Between Wednesday afternoon classes, Ezra weaved among standing and moving students in the hallways in much the same way that he would penetrate the defensive secondary on the playing field. But among the commotion and clamor of voices, one figure got his attention, even without speaking. Coach Hadoff stood in his classroom doorway, face full of business and gesturing with an upraised hand.

Ezra knew what that meant. He skirted a cluster of students and took three quick steps to cross the hall. "What's up, Coach?"

"Wilson, we need to talk. Soon."

"Talk? It's January. I've been listening to recruiters for more than three months. Is this going to be more of the usual?"

Hadoff offered up a wry laugh. "The usual? No, not this time. I've got a proposition for you, one that might interest you for a change. Something for your own good."

"For my own good, eh? We've been down that road. Several times."

"Hey, watch it! I don't appreciate your attitude toward your future, given your abilities. You don't know what's best for you. I do." Hadoff was no longer laughing.

"All right if you say so. When should I stop in?"

"Tomorrow after school?"

"Yep. I'll come to your office."

"Good. See you then. And I told you, this is something new. Don't be late." Coach Hadoff stepped back into his classroom. Ezra turned and continued to his next class. He knew the purpose of Hadoff's summons. They had been through it all before and he would not be changing his mind on the subject. Poor Coach didn't get it.

But he had said that this was something new. Ezra was curious. He would at least give the guy a chance.

"Close the door behind you, Wilson."

Ezra pressed the door closed and turned. Yep, there he was, another visitor; nothing new here. Coach had several times invited him to meet with college football program recruiters. He knew the routine. Heaps of praise followed by a predictable series of questions. Finally, the promises. But this meeting, Coach had said, would be different.

Ezra discerned that difference upon entering the room. A stiffness. Heaviness. Coach in his usual place behind his desk, but this time leaning back in his chair, legs stretched out and hands clasped behind his head. He recognized that posture; Coach was feeling anxious but trying his best to look relaxed. Whatever was in store, the stakes were high for him.

To the right, Coach's guest. Wearing a navy-blue suit, white shirt, and tie—studying Ezra in the same way he might appraise a trophy, or an expensive sports car. He was tall and lean, probably in his late 50s or early 60s. Hair that shined unnaturally in the fluorescent lighting. Maybe a former athlete who still enjoyed a game of basketball or tennis, or at least worked out regularly. Wing-tipped shoes, cufflinks, strong cologne. The smell of money.

"Ezra Wilson, I'd like you to meet Mr. Lance Boyer." Coach tilted his head toward the navy-blue suit man, who stood and stuck out his hand while offering a smile that was too broad. Ezra nodded and shook hands.

"Please have a seat." Coach pointed at the chair across from Boyer.

Ezra glanced out the broad office window to snow-covered landscape and trees, glistening in the twilight. Football season was long over, but the aggressive college recruiters were still at work, competing for the best that the region's high schools had to offer. He was no stranger to their ways and had learned to spot them when they stepped onto school grounds.

This Mr. Boyer was not a recruiter; his clothes and his attitude spoke otherwise. Coach had called the meeting and would have to make the first move.

But Boyer opened the discussion. "Tell me what your plans are after you graduate." Right down to business. No small talk or words of praise or flattery.

"Sure, Mr. Boyer. I'll be attending the University."

"An excellent choice. And call me Lance, please."

"Ok, Lance. I'll start at the U next fall, to study mechanical engineering."

"And you'll play football of course. The way I see it, you've got a good chance of making first string, even as a freshman." Boyer spoke differently, not as a recruiter but matter-of-factly. Not a plea or a question, but as a statement of fact. A foregone conclusion. Had he and Coach already sealed a deal?

"So, I've been told. But I'm not going to play football in college. My focus will be on academics. After I've earned my master's, I'll pursue my engineering career, and then enroll in seminary. My objective is to work in a profession that will also allow me to pastor a church."

Boyer's face tightened, and he looked over at Hadoff. The coach raised his eyebrows and lifted one corner of his mouth, a look which seemed to say, "I told you so."

But Boyer was undaunted. "Young man, it's interesting that you would say such a thing. You're a natural athlete. From what I understand, you seem to have the ability to sail right through defenses. You have an unusual gift in that respect. You can't let all that go."

"Thank you for the compliment, but my heart's not in *all that*."

"I find that hard to believe." Boyer's voice held an edge.

"Lance, don't get me wrong. I love playing football and will always love the game. But playing college football is a huge commitment of time and attention and effort. It doesn't line up with what I want. My long-term goals."

"But how can you throw away such an opportunity? You're young, maybe not qualified to make such a decision. Are you sure you've thought this through?"

Growing irritated with Boyer's condescending tone, he ignored the question. "Lance, I'm curious. You don't look like a recruiter to me. Why are you here?"

Lance looked at Hadoff, and then back at Ezra.

"You are correct. I am not a recruiter. But I believe I offer you far more than a mere college scholarship and opportunity to be part of a Big Ten Conference squad."

"And that would be…?"

"I'm the vice-president of marketing and promotion at Springier Athletics. I imagine you've heard of us."

"Yes, I have. Athletic gear and accessories. An up-and-coming company. I own some of your stuff."

"Glad to hear that. Springier is a young company, six years in the business but growing. We're establishing a stellar reputation among high school and college athletic programs and are hoping to break into the professional arena."

"I'm happy to hear of your success. But what does that have to do with me?"

"You're a bright and sensible young man with exceptional ability. I'm here today to talk business with you, specifically product promotion and endorsement. In a way that puts your face out in front and money in your pocket. I'm talking about far more than your college athletic career and scholarship money."

Okay, admittedly, this was different. But there had to be a cost. "As long as?" he asked.

"Provided you play football."

"Hold on." Ezra formed a time-out motion with his hands. "Product endorsement? We're talking collegiate athletics here, not the NFL."

"No, we're not talking about the NFL—not yet. But I hope you understand that you've got a good shot at being recruited after college. And, who knows? You might even get a shot at an endorsement contract while still in college. I keep my ear to the ground with the NCAA on such issues, and we are hopeful that the landscape will change with regard to college student athletes' rights and status with promotional opportunities."

"Interesting. But what you're talking about is speculative at this point. Probably several years off."

"Maybe so. But we at Springier like what we see in you now, and we are willing to take the chance of making a contract. And we can offer plenty of incentives up front if you will work with us—incentives outside of the specific jurisdiction of the NCAA or the University."

A business deal. That was the end game for Boyer, maybe even for Coach. Was he going to get a cut of this action? Ezra looked over at his coach. It was no secret at school that Curt Hadoff struggled to support his wife and four children on his coaching and teaching salary. There was also the unsubstantiated rumor that he had a gambling problem, and that was why his wife was forced to work full-time. The man would not be above finding other ways to raise needed cash.

Ezra turned his attention back to Boyer. "You speak of incentives. Like what?"

"I'm not yet at liberty to discuss that. That would all come after a commitment on your part. Once you're on board, we'll talk specifics."

Ezra hesitated, considering the man's words. Plenty of incentives. Mr. Boyer's offer might deserve at least some initial consideration after all. He could still pursue his academics. And his parents would be spared a large financial burden.

But he would not be pressured.

"Okay, Lance." He stood. "I've heard what you've said today. I will think about it, but that's it for today."

"Okay. Thank you for giving us your time. And, once again, I wouldn't be wasting my time with you here today if I didn't believe that you were destined for greatness. I'm sure that your coach here would agree with me. Keep that in mind."

"Thank you. I will do that." He picked up his coat and left.

The door closed behind Ezra, and Hadoff leaned forward in his seat. "I told you that Wilson would be a tough one to crack. He's got an unusual measure of self-awareness and resolve for a kid his age."

"Hey, Curt, have faith." Boyer stood and collected his belongings. "I know a good investment when I see it. We're not done here. And he did say he would think about it."

"True," Hadoff conceded.

"I've worked with young men like Wilson before," Boyer said. "They can never turn down the opportunity to get paid to play. Don't give up. I've got a secret weapon."

Gabe Wilson crawled backward out from under the kitchen sink cabinet and raised himself up. One greasy hand held a section of drain pipe. Still on his knees, he reached around and pressed his free hand into the small of his back, grimacing. "I'm getting too old to be crawling around on the floor like this. Next time we're calling a plumber."

Ezra dropped his backpack onto a kitchen chair and turned to fill a drinking glass from the refrigerator door tap.

"Hand me some more paper towels. And tell me about your meeting with Coach yesterday. Sorry we couldn't catch up last night."

"Well, Dad, the so-called recruiter that I was supposed to meet turned out to be some promoter. From Springier Athletics."

"Huh, no kidding." Gabe's face was covered in sweat, but bore its characteristic calm while Ezra related to him the exchange in Coach Hadoff's office. Gabe displayed little emotion; as a family attorney, he was accustomed to conflict and confrontation, and generally found his talented son's occasional spars with college recruiters to be amusing.

"Sounds like the hounds continue to up the ante with you, don't they?"

"No kidding. This is getting ridiculous."

"So… have you changed your mind?"

"No. But I'll admit that this guy talks a different talk than the rest of them. And he looks different, all decked-out in a nice suit, like what you wear when you make your court appearances."

"Imagine that!" Gabe disappeared back into the sink cabinet. "Son, I hate to cut this conversation short, but I promised your mother that I would have this drain replaced before dinner. I'm about there if you'll give me a couple of minutes."

"Sure. We'll continue then." Ezra picked up his backpack.

Ezra looked forward to dinnertime when the whole family could sit down and eat together. There would be stories, laughs, and wisdom served up with the food. Dad would share animated accounts of the drama and antics of his clients, both in and out of the courtroom. Grandma Lois would recount experiences and lessons from her own long life.

Recently, Ezra had taken a greater role in those dinner table discussions, prompted by his encounters with the various college recruiters that Coach was introducing. He'd witnessed and analyzed a variety of their sales tactics and other persuasive measures and enjoyed being able to contribute stories and perspectives of his own.

Tonight, all five family members were present, and the topic of conversation would again be a study in human nature.

"I look at it this way. It all boils down to what we've talked about before. Intrinsic versus extrinsic motivation." With a forkful of meatloaf hovering over his plate, Gabe addressed the dinner table—his wife Trish; Ezra; younger brother Anthony; and Trish's mother Lois. "Mom and I have done our best to raise you boys to be intrinsically motivated. That is what will help and protect you in life."

"Yes, the world is full of good people, and there are some not-so-good ones." Trish spoke in tandem with her husband. "Both of you boys are bright and talented. People notice that, and there will always be those who come along and dangle a carrot in front of you."

"Yes, boys. Take it from one who has learned the hard way." Lois dabbed at her mouth with her napkin. "People are human, and subject to human nature. They look out for themselves, set you up on a pedestal of someone else's making, for their own benefit. That's when you have to know who you are and what you stand for. Hey, Gabe" —she pointed across the table— "please pass me the carrots."

"Your mother and grandmother are both right, as usual." Gabe handed off the carrots with one hand and reached for a bowl of au gratin potatoes with the other. "Flattery can be a dangerous pitfall. And so can greed." He laughed. "I should know. Flattery and greed both help provide job security for me."

Ezra stiffened, wondering if his dad's last comments were directed toward him. "I *have* been careful with Coach and Mr. Boyer. All I told them was that I would *think* about what they offered."

"That part is fine. But there's one thing you said that concerns me," Gabe said. "This whole matter of incentives. Especially that Mr. Boyer wouldn't elaborate. When I hear that, I smell a rat. Either something downright illegal or unethical, or at least operating in some gray area regarding NCAA or University policies."

"Yeah, that bothered me, too. And I'm even wondering about Coach's role in all of this. I wouldn't be surprised if he gets a financial kickback. It's common knowledge around school that he runs tight on funds from time to time."

Gabe shook his head. "I feel sorry for the guy in that respect. He has his own issues and makes his own decisions. We can't control what he does. But we can choose to protect ourselves. Guard our convictions, our integrity."

Trish spoke up. "That's where your dad and I are willing to step back and let you be an adult. This situation with Coach Hadoff and this Mr. Boyer presents an excellent practice drill. We'll let you handle it."

She cast a warning look at Anthony. "Don't worry, your day is coming."

"Thanks, Mom." He made a face. "Just what I want to hear."

"Practice drills," Ezra echoed, scraping the last bits of food from his plate. "It seems that lately I've been getting a lot of them."

"Well, one thing you can count on," Gabe said to Ezra. "These Springier folks and Coach Hadoff have got you in their crosshairs. They won't waste any time in reaching out to you again, and my gut tells me that they won't be entirely forthcoming. Stay alert and remember who you are."

Ezra trotted out to the front of the school building. Friday evening, and he was eager to get home. Tonight, a Gopher hockey game; he had barely enough time for an early dinner before his buddies picked him up.

As he reached the curb, Coach Hadoff's Toyota sedan pulled up on the far side of the front drive, and the passenger window came down. "Wilson!" he called out. His hand beckoned from within.

"Hey, Coach, what's up?" He wound his way among students and between two busses to reach the car.

"You taking the bus home tonight?"

"Yep."

"Here, hop in. I'll run you home. Need to talk for a minute."

"Sure, thanks!" Ezra noticed Coach's facial expression. The man looked agitated; the topic for discussion must be critical. Nevertheless, he pulled the door open and jumped in, and they took off.

Several minutes of total silence prevailed before Coach spoke. "How was school today?"

Coach asking about his day? He never cared about that before. He must be nervous.

"Fine overall. Calculus has been a bear, but I'll nail it. I've got to if I'm going to major in engineering in college."

"Well, everyone says that if you can handle Thatcher's class, you should be able to handle anything they can throw at you in college."

"I've heard that too. I hope they're right."

This is odd. Coach had said he needed to talk about something, but so far there had been nothing but small talk. They were more than halfway home. What would cause him to behave this way? He'd better get around to it soon.

At the next intersection the coach turned left instead of right.

"Hey, I thought you were running me home."

"I am. I promise. One quick stop on the way, and I'll still get you home faster than the bus would."

That didn't add up. Coach had always been his determined and cunning self, a trait which helped him to become a successful, winning coach. But he had never pulled a 'bait 'n switch' move like this before.

"Hey, don't worry. It's no big deal." Coach must have discerned his thoughts. "I'd like you to meet someone."

The remainder of the ride was endured in silence, Ezra mentally kicking himself for having been deceived so easily. Whatever was in store couldn't be legit, not the way things were playing out.

After several more turns, the Toyota pulled to a stop at an address that Ezra had visited once before: the Hadoff home.

Lance Boyer looked up into the rear-view mirror. "Looks like our friends have arrived. Are you ready?"

"Always." The young woman unbuckled her seatbelt and twisted around to where she could watch a silver sedan pull into the driveway behind them. Then she turned back to Lance, noting the strained look on his face. "Honey, quit worrying. I've done my research."

"Good. No slip-ups… like last time. That was embarrassing."

"Hey!" The nerve of him calling her out this way! She was not a child. "You put me into a very sticky situation last week. Way beyond what you had prepared me for."

"Maybe so. But you're supposed to be able to roll with the unexpected. That's why I pay you the big bucks. If you had stuck to the script, there wouldn't have been an issue."

"Lance, that was a poor excuse for a script, and you know it. It was my own quick wits that saved the deal in the end. I demand more respect from you if we're going to continue to be partners."

"Your partnering with me is a privilege. Don't forget that."

"A privilege? Hardly. Maybe I need to have a little chat with your wife or your daughters about what you call a privilege. They might not look at it that way."

Lance's demeanor changed. "Okay, Sylvia. No need to threaten me."

"Then quit being a jerk."

"Okay, dear. I apologize for our misunderstanding. But we've got a job to do this afternoon. Keep in mind that for the next half-hour you're a marketing executive and a former U of M sorority girl. Nothing beyond that. Not a professional model, not the dean's wife, not a semi-pro golfer…you get the idea."

"Hey, can the attitude! I hardly expect a high school kid and his coach to grill me the way that those junior college officials and their board members did."

"You're right, dear. I'm sorry. This should be a breeze." Boyer opened his car door and pulled his briefcase from the back seat. "Here we go."

Parked in his driveway, Hadoff opened his door, then turned back. "Ten minutes. I promise. Then I'll run you home, still ahead of the bus." He climbed out, then stopped and called back over his shoulder. "You'll thank me later."

Ezra then noticed the black Lincoln sedan parked at the front curb. The car's front doors opened simultaneously. Waving toward the Lincoln, Hadoff led the way to the front door, unlocked it and stepped inside. The house looked unoccupied; evidently Coach's wife and kids were still out. Once inside, Ezra looked back to see a man and woman coming up the front walk.

"Come on in, everyone." Hadoff threw off his coat and moved about the front room, turning on lights and closing the front drapes. The two other visitors stepped into the light, Lance Boyer, in the lead and carrying a briefcase.

Not him again! What was going on with Lance and Coach? This time at the Hadoff residence, away from school grounds. Away from any possibility of outside observation.

Behind Lance was a woman. A young, stunningly attractive woman who pulled off her fur coat, revealing a skirt that came to well above her knees, despite single-digit temperatures. She removed her scarf and shook out her hair while looking Ezra up and down.

"Ezra. Coach Hadoff. Please meet my associate, Sylvia Masters."

"Ezra, I'm so glad to finally get to meet you." She crossed the room and grasped Ezra's hand in both of hers. "Lance has bragged about you, and I had to get my eyes on you for myself."

"Uh, thank you. Pleased to meet you too." He steeled himself, his thoughts reeling over this turn of events, the way in which Coach had snared him for these wolves. How could he ever trust the man again?

Lance eased himself into one of two matching chairs and indicated for Hadoff to take the other. That left the sofa; Ezra sat on one end, and Sylvia, after great ceremony of smoothing and adjusting her blouse and skirt, sat alongside him.

Lance spoke first. "I asked your coach to bring you here this afternoon so that Sylvia could offer her own perspective on your future with University of Minnesota football."

"Yes." Sylvia leaned toward him and placed her hand on his forearm. "I work with Lance at Springier. But I'm also an alumnus of the University. In fact, I was a sorority girl there and am well acquainted with the University's athletic programs. And I know several of the players personally."

"Okay." Ezra's insides began to squirm. A high school star athlete, he was accustomed to the attention of his female peers, but this woman was operating at a whole other level. She was probably six or eight years older than him and looked way too comfortable in her role.

"Lance and I are asking you to at least give us a chance to work with you. I believe he has given you an overview of what we offer. I want to be an encouragement to you. To be sure that you don't sell yourself short."

"Sell myself short? In what way?"

"You intend to pursue a degree in engineering, am I right?"

"Yes, ma'am."

She flinched at his use of the term. "Please, call me Sylvia."

"Okay. Yes, Sylvia."

"And then go into the ministry? Correct?"

"Yes."

"Well, I certainly respect your admirable goals. I can assure you of that. But I feel that you should at least give us a fair shot at helping you discover who you are, your true capabilities. We are professionals at what we do, and we know of your potential, for both college football and beyond. You have the ability that most young athletes like you dream of."

"Yes, I keep hearing that."

"And campus life for a star athlete like you comes with extra benefits, the kinds that you don't read about in the brochures. I don't think that I need to elaborate."

"No, I get it." His nervousness increased with each nudge, each gentle squeeze of Sylvia's hand on his arm. For once, he didn't have the upper hand in the conversation. Whoever this Lance and Sylvia were, they were operating on a much different level than had those he'd encountered before.

And…how long had he been here? Coach had promised ten minutes. But then, Coach had already proved that he couldn't be trusted.

Sylvia leaned in, her warm breath and the scent of sweet perfume brushing the side of his face. "What are you afraid of? Afraid of learning the truth about yourself perhaps?"

"But I do know what I want. I figured that out a couple of years ago, and it hasn't changed."

"Here's the way I see things." She shifted closer, tightening her grip. "You won't commit to something—even with no strings attached—simply because you *think* you're settled on who you are and what you want. But you're really giving in to fear."

Fear?

The notion had never occurred to him. Was it all about fear, and not a humble resolve? Had he been kidding himself about what he thought he wanted? Maybe Lance and Sylvia and Coach were right after all—that he was underselling himself. Maybe he was indeed entitled to the recognition and benefits that they had described.

Sylvia looked at Lance, who leaned down and extracted a sheaf of papers from his briefcase. He handed them to her.

"Ezra," she said, caressing the pages in her hands. "You are eighteen years old, correct?"

He could again feel her warm breath against the side of his face. "Yes."

"Then, if you would simply sign this letter of intent, we could get started with processing the contractual agreements. Again, like I said, no strings attached at this point. But this smooths the way forward. And I believe that you will begin to understand the wisdom of your decision to work with us."

Sylvia could be right. There was no harm in giving it a chance. He was not going to allow fear to dictate his decisions.

She leaned in closer, so that her face was inches from his own. "I will be working with you personally, every step of the way. You and I will become both good friends and partners in this venture. Do you understand me?"

His thoughts went out to the playing field. To the snap followed by quarterback Davidson's shout. His own plunge forward through the defenders, barely feeling their touch. Like walking through walls.

He looked over at Coach. The man had promised this wouldn't take long. How long had they all been here? Thirty minutes? He was running out of time. A decision had to be made.

"Okay," he breathed, heart pounding. "Where do I sign?"

"What happened?"

The question was not accusatory. To Ezra, his dad appeared neither unhappy nor angry, but curious. He was an attorney after all. With the ability to keep his thoughts to himself, not betrayed by facial expressions or body language. Stretched out, fully reclined in the family room with an opened novel lying face-down across his stomach and slippers on his feet, his having just returned home from a four-day business trip away.

"You found the copy of the letter, Dad?" The question was rhetorical; once back home from the meeting at Coach's house, he had purposefully laid his copy of the Springier signed letter of intent on his father's desk, his part in initiating another father-to-son talk at the appropriate time.

Ezra's initial sense of accomplishment and satisfaction at the conclusion of the fast-paced, 25-minute meeting in the Hadoff living room had dissolved during his trip home. Even Coach himself had been silent and withdrawn during the drive, probably feeling guilty over what he knew he had done to his star player.

The meeting with Boyer and Masters had concluded abruptly. Once the letter was signed, Coach came to life, bounced up from his chair, and ushered the pair out of the house. Then wasted no time in getting Ezra into his car. The reason was obvious. It was nearing five o'clock. The school bus would soon be dropping Coach's children off, and his wife would get home from work. Likely none of them had any idea of what had transpired in their living room.

But what hurt was that Ezra had done exactly what he had promised himself that he would never do: cave.

In signing the letter, he had compromised his own rules; let his parents down; let his faithful grandmother down. All because a couple of slick operators had cornered and outwitted him in the matter of a few minutes.

The sound of his dad's voice jarred his thoughts back to the present. "Yes, I found it. Right where you left it for me. Hence, my question: What happened?"

Ezra busied himself hanging his jacket in the closet, unlacing his snow-covered shoes, and emptying out his backpack. He was resigned to, but in no hurry for, the inevitable and forthcoming "life-lesson."

"I got took, Dad. Bulldozed."

"How did you 'get took' as you say?"

"You should have been there. Coach had scheduled the meeting and pulled a fast one to get me there. Then turned everything over to the two snakes from Springier. Mr. Boyer did his part, which I had expected. But his partner, a Miss Masters, was the one who put the finishing touches on me. She was young and hot-looking and knew all the right words and moves. And I was in a hurry to get it over with and come home. All in all, a bad combination of circumstances. And I caved."

Gabe reached down and picked up the single sheet of paper from where he had set it on the floor beside the recliner. He scanned the document, probably for Ezra's benefit; undoubtedly, he had earlier read through it with his attorney eyes. "Well, if this is all that you signed, no harm done. If you're not interested in pursuing this, I can make it all go away, like that" —he snapped his fingers— "But I'll probably let you handle that little matter yourself. A good learning opportunity."

"I thought so. Thank you for not getting upset."

"Upset? So, you slipped up under pressure from a couple of seasoned professionals. Helped along by your own deceitful coach. In this case, a cheap lesson." Gabe raised up the recliner to where he could more squarely face his son. "But I want to get to the bottom of what happened in that meeting. What exactly led you to sign this letter against your better judgment?"

"Well, for starters I can tell you that I haven't changed my mind about my plans."

"Okay. Why do you say that?"

"Because, deep down, I still know who I am and what I want."

"So, if you know 'who you are and what you want', what did they say that got you to give in?"

"Man, I've wrestled with that for the past couple of days. Then I figured it out. It started with the usual dose of attention and flattery, this time with an attractive young woman in the mix. They took advantage of my tight time schedule and pushed me to make a quick decision. They talked up the benefits, the acclaim and so on. All the usual pride and greed bait."

"You've faced that before, Son."

"But what got me in the end was when they played the fear card. They told me that my unwillingness to cooperate was due to fear. My fear of discovering who I am and what I deserve. They accused me of selling myself short, being afraid to even try."

"Ooh. That was slick on their part. Well played, I have to admit."

"Unfortunately, it worked this time."

"Then, what is your takeaway from this experience?"

"Oh, it all comes down to what you've taught me all my life. Know thyself."

"And…?"

"If I am secure and satisfied in being Ezra Wilson—nothing more and nothing less—then I can't be bought."

"Well said."

Matthew 5:5 (KJV)
Blessed are the meek: for they shall inherit the earth.

Matthew 5:5 (AMP)
Blessed [inwardly peaceful, spiritually secure, worthy of respect] are the gentle [the kind-hearted, the sweet-spirited, the self-controlled], for they will inherit the earth.

Matthew 5:5 (MSG)
You're blessed when you're content with just who you are—no more, no less. That's the moment you find yourselves proud owners of everything that can't be bought.

MILES

The image was startling, otherworldly. Elongated eyeballs, nearly touching each other on a tall, rectangular head; wide, distorted cheeks; a flattened nose, gaping mouth and pointy chin. Something that one might encounter in a sci-fi movie.

No sense in trying to check my appearance in this thing! Miles Moore laughed self-consciously. Leave it to a toy and novelty company to place a fun house mirror right in front of the elevator doors.

When had he last looked at himself in one of these? After making several faces at himself, he turned to look reverently upon the blazing red and yellow logo and name, comprised of hundreds of tiles embedded into a frosty glass wall to his left. A name he had cherished from childhood: *Toyzania*.

He smoothed his hair and snugged up his tie one last time before entering the doors at the end of the hallway.

A cheerful-looking woman wearing a pink scarf emblazoned with cartoon stick figures greeted him. "Good morning, Mr. Moore. We've been expecting you."

A giant panda bear, probably eight feet in height, watched him through unblinking eyes from one corner. Across the room a lighted case displayed a castle constructed of colorful building blocks. Several photos of children and their toys adorned the walls.

The woman stood and ushered him down a short hallway to another set of double doors. He couldn't help but notice the words printed on a brass wall placard: You don't have to be a child to work here, but it helps.

Miles stepped into a large conference room, and the woman pressed the doors shut behind him.

Before him, a gleaming mahogany table with twelve unoccupied chairs lined in precision along its sides. Along the left wall, more framed photographs of children at play with various kinds of toys and games. To the right, floor-to-ceiling glass panes affording a stunning view of the Chicago skyline and the Lake Michigan waterfront, twenty-seven stories below.

His gaze traveled along the length of the table to its far end, beholding a man who neither spoke nor moved. The eyes, however, were watching. Charles Zane.

Even seated, Toyzania's founder and CEO appeared quite tall, with a commanding presence felt from across the room. A long lean face and full head of white hair and wearing a navy-blue suit with a yellow necktie displaying the faces of cartoon characters.

Miles found his voice. "Good morning, Mr. Zane. Thank you for inviting me here."

Mr. Zane nodded slightly and extended his hand, indicating that Miles was to take the seat next to his own. "Good morning. Miles Moore it is, correct?"

"Yes, sir."

"Miles, my time today is limited, so let me get right to the point. You have been vetted by my team, hence this meeting. I have a question for you: why do you wish to work for Toyzania?"

Boy, this guy doesn't waste time in getting to the point! "Mr. Zane, because I love your products and what you do and how your products delight children and adults. As a kid, I played with Trixie puppets and Zany magic sets and wore your costumes for Halloween."

The white-haired head nodded.

"And," Miles continued. "This position appears to dovetail exactly with my education and work experience credentials. We would make a good team."

"I see." The man placed his hand onto a folder lying on the table. "As you know, following your second interview we contacted your references and did our own checking on your background, which we have found acceptable. Twenty-seven years old with an MBA and several years of experience under your belt. A fine lineup of reference sources, a couple of whom I know personally. It does appear that you are worthy of further consideration."

Miles nodded, waiting. Was the other shoe about to drop?

"Let's get back to my first question. Why do you want to work here?"

"Mr. Zane, this would be the fulfillment of a dream for me. I would serve you well and feel proud to be here. I believe in what you do; it is personal to me."

"Okay, very well. You are aware of the critical nature of the position for which you have applied. Therefore, before this process goes any further, I need to get to know you, not only from your resume or from what others say about you, but what's inside, what's in here." He patted his hand over his heart. "To that end you will do something for me."

He handed Miles a plain white, sealed envelope. "We're finished here for today. Take this with you, but don't open it until you leave the building. We'll be in touch."

Mr. Zane stood, indicating that the meeting was over. It had lasted less than ten minutes.

Miles was eager to open the mysterious envelope but waited until he had exited the building and walked to his car in a nearby parking ramp. Sliding into the driver's seat, he slit open the envelope, and pulled out a single sheet of paper with this typewritten message:

```
July 6, 1999
Mr. Moore:

Thank you for meeting me today and for
your interest in Toyzania. Before we
continue any further, please do the fol-
lowing: Take this letter to the Acme
Costume Store on East Grand Avenue. Give
it to Marcia who works there and ask her
to give you your costume and sign board.

You will wear both it and the sign board,
stand in front of the Toyzania re-
tail shop out on Navy Pier on Wednesday
from 9 AM until noon, and greet all
passers-by.

At noon you may return everything to
Marcia. Don't worry about anything else,
and don't be late. Marcia is expecting
you.

Sincerely,
Charles M. Zane
```

Miles's jaw dropped and he tossed the paper onto the floor. *What is this? Some kind of stupid joke? I didn't sign up to be an idiot!* On top of that, Wednesday was tomorrow; there was no time to waste! The glow he had been feeling from his brief meeting fizzled. He fumed, pulling his tie from around his neck and flinging it onto the seat beside him. Then he gunned the engine and made his way back to his apartment.

Early afternoon found Miles in his running shorts and lacing up his shoes. No better way to deal with anger and frustration than to run it off. He locked the door, scrambled down two flights of stairs, and took off down the street at a steady pace.

One hour later he returned, considerably calmer, in part from the physical exertion and in part because he had processed the issue at hand. Okay, he would swallow his pride and go to the costume shop. He still had time to get there this afternoon, even if it meant another drive into downtown. He did want the job after all.

"Hi, Marcia?"

"Yes, may I help you?"

"Yes, Miles Moore. From Toyzania. I believe you have something for me?"

"Ahh, yes. Moore. The court jester costume. And the sign board." Marcia disappeared through a doorway and reappeared with a plastic-wrapped outfit on a hanger and a pair of rectangular sheets of paneling, held together at one end by straps. Oddly, Marcia didn't ask any questions, and Miles suspected that she was in on this escapade.

Back in his car, he tore open the plastic enough to extract the costume's cap. Pink and green and pointed with several bells hanging from the tip. Even his careful handling of the cap caused their clanging.

"Man, I must seriously want this job," he whispered. "Tomorrow morning is going to be an adventure."

Wednesday morning out on Navy Pier passed slowly, though not for lack of activity or attention. Fair skies meant that pedestrian traffic was heavy with sightseers as well as those who lived or worked in the area. Men, women, children, and dogs.

Miles frequently sneaked looks at his watch, urging the time to hurry. At precisely twelve noon, he pulled off his pointy cap and hurried to his car in a nearby parking ramp to retrieve his regular clothes. From there to a public restroom to change his outfit. Finally, back to the costume shop; he couldn't wait to hand it off.

Predictably, the morning's assignment had been quite humiliating, reactions ranging from his being ignored, to polite condescension, to laughter and jeering. A group of young boys had taunted him and tried to steal his cap; an old man seemed to feel sorry for him and gave him a dollar; still others approached him asking for money. The hours had dragged on, but Miles maintained his composure and fully complied with his instructions, suspecting that he was being watched.

"Do I need to pay you for this?" he asked Marcia.

"No, that's all taken care of. However..." Here, a sly smile. "I have this for you. Take it outside before you open it." Another plain white envelope.

This time Miles waited until he had gotten home before opening the envelope. Another typewritten message from Mr. Zane:

```
July 7, 1999
Mr. Moore:

Thank you for your obedience to my
first instruction; you exhibited humble
character.

This Thursday evening, the Salvation
Army will be serving meals to about 150
of our homeless citizens in the downtown
area. You will arrive at the Salvation
Army building on North Desplaines Street
by 5 PM. Please report to Mr. Simmons.
```

```
You will help set up and serve. Cleanup
is afterwards, including the kitchen,
the dining area, and the restrooms. You
should be finished up by 10:30 or
so. Thank you for your service.

Sincerely,
Charles M. Zane

P.S. No one ever accused me of being
conventional
```

Here we go again. He dropped the note onto his desk. When would the craziness end? He would have to reschedule tomorrow's tennis game with his friend Tony and spend the evening in a part of town where he had never been. That is, if he wanted the job. Miles punched out a brief text message to Tony.

Thursday evening's tour of duty was much less humiliating than Wednesday's had been, but physically harder and less pleasant work. Supervisor Art Simmons was a kind man, and Miles found satisfaction in scooping mashed potatoes onto plates for the hungry crowd that passed through the line for more than two hours. But cleanup afterwards was almost more than he could stomach, having had no idea of how homeless people took full advantage of available restrooms. He felt saturated—even infected—by the mixture of filth encountered and the cleaning chemicals needed and couldn't wait to get home to throw all his clothes into the wash and take a long, steaming hot shower. By 10 PM, lights had been extinguished and volunteers were exiting the building.

Art approached and stuck out his hand. "Thank you, Miles. You've been a great help here tonight."

"You're welcome. I'll admit that I wasn't too keen on the idea at first, but it turned out to be okay for me."

"Glad to hear it." Art paused. "Hey, have you got five minutes?"

"Sure."

Art pulled out a couple of folding chairs. "Before you leave, I want to tell you about Charlie."

"You mean Mr. Zane. The man that sent me out here as part of my employment application process."

"Yep, that's Charlie all right. I've known him for about fifteen years, and that guy has his own style, his own way of doing business. People have always said that his last name appropriately describes him. You know, zany."

"Well, I don't know him well enough to say that about him, but I agree that he plays by his own rules."

"There's one thing you need to understand about Charlie Zane. He may be in the toy business, but he's also in the people business. He grows people. In his own way."

"Whew! I can tell you he's grown me already, both yesterday and today."

"I believe you're getting the picture. I can promise you that, assuming you land this job, Charlie will stretch you. You will learn your job and about Toyzania. More importantly, you will learn about yourself, your true capabilities. That's how he operates. Yes, he cares about toys. But he cares more about people, especially those who work for him."

"Well, whatever he's doing, he's made a success of it."

"Right. All that to say that Charlie knows what he's doing and doesn't waste his time. You may not understand everything, but he wouldn't be putting you through your paces like this if he didn't see potential in you. So, take heart."

"Thank you for letting me know. That helps."

Art stood. "It's late, and my wife and kids are probably wondering where I am. I need to get going. Glad to have met you, Miles. And anytime you wish to serve, you are welcome to come back. We are here every Thursday night, and we can always use some help." He plucked something from his coat pocket: a white envelope.

"Here, please take this."

Miles grabbed it, thanked the man, and departed. Great! Another envelope!

Back at home, he withdrew the expected single sheet of paper to find the following:

```
July 8, 1999
Mr. Moore:

Thank you for your obedience so far. You
have proved yourself to be a hard work-
er, even with unpleasant assignments.

This Saturday our state's middle school
spelling bee quarterfinals will be held
at Potter Auditorium. Among the contes-
tants will be my granddaughter, Kassie,
a 7th-grader.

I need you to attend the competition,
which begins at 9 AM and will last
throughout most of the day. Your assign-
ment there is to write down the names
of every contestant, along with every
spelling word dictated throughout the
contest. At the conclusion of the compe-
tition, turn your list in to Dr. Edith
Phillips, one of the judges.

Sincerely,
Charles M. Zane
```

A spelling bee? All day Saturday? Miles Moore, an aspiring executive, sitting among a bunch of mothers and fathers with nothing to do other than waste a Saturday in a school auditorium.

Then he checked himself. *Okay, I've been warned. This is the way it's going to be if I want this job.*

Miles entered the auditorium shortly before the nine o'clock starting time on Saturday. The number of audience members was sparse, most likely parents, grandparents, and teachers. Who else in their right minds would choose to spend a Saturday listening to school children spell words?

He took a seat in the third row, center section, pleased to find that it was padded and would recline. At least he would be comfortable, although staying awake might be a challenge. He opened a brand new spiral bound notebook in his lap.

The program began within a few minutes and progressed throughout the morning without a break. Mr. Zane's granddaughter was indeed a contestant, and represented herself well, but was eliminated from the competition by mid-morning.

Periodically, Miles scanned the small crowd, looking to see if Mr. Zane himself was in attendance, but did not spot him. During the noon lunch break, Miles stepped outside to buy a hamburger and a soda from a nearby food truck and sat in the grass to eat and give his mind a break. Over the past three hours he had filled four pages with his list of names and spelling words. It was going to be a long afternoon.

By four-thirty the final contestants had faced off, and the winners were recognized. A brief ceremony on stage followed and pictures were taken. The moderator then officially brought things to a close by thanking everybody involved for being there and encouraging them to attend the semi-finals in two weeks.

Not me! Miles thought.

As people dispersed a small crew appeared from the wings to reset the stage. Miles sought out the four judges, who were standing at the back of the auditorium.

"Dr. Phillips?" he called, and a distinguished looking middle-aged woman turned.

"You must be Mr. Moore," she said. "I believe you have something for me."

Miles gratefully handed off the notebook. He had obediently jumped through three of Zane's hoops. This had to be the end of things.

But that was not to be. The woman pulled a white envelope from her pocket and handed it to him. He started to step away but turned back. "Dr. Phillips, I have one question for you."

"Sure."

"You must know Charles Zane."

"Oh, indeed."

"Was he here today? I can't imagine him missing out on his granddaughter's event, but I haven't seen him at all."

"Oh, I haven't seen him either. But that doesn't mean he's not here."

Thanking her, Miles exited the auditorium. Back in his car, he tore open the envelope.

```
July 10, 1999
Mr. Moore:

Well done thus far. You have exhibited
patience and obedience, even when things
don't seem to make sense.
```

Your final assignment will test your
courage. A certain Mr. Theodore Crenshaw
owes me some money. He is obstinate,
difficult to work with, and I have neither the time nor the inclination to
deal with him personally.

You will locate Mr. Crenshaw and pay a
visit to him this Monday at about 9 AM
to collect what is owed. You absolutely
must succeed at this task. Do not under any circumstances leave him until he
gives you the money. He has it, and he
knows that he owes it to me. You must
simply compel him to do what is right.

Sincerely,
Charles M. Zane

Reading Mr. Zane's latest instructions, Miles felt a chill run up and down his spine. This was taking things up a couple of notches. Scenes of heated arguments followed by violence, gleaned from action and suspense movies, came to mind. This could be dangerous! Who was this Theodore Crenshaw? Was he a thug or merely a harmless bully? And why isn't Mr. Zane himself willing to take this guy on?

Monday was two days away, not a lot of time to prepare. Miles sped home, grabbed his laptop, and typed in the name. No difficulty here; the first listing to pop up identified Theodore J. Crenshaw as CFO of Marquart Novelties, Incorporated, a regional chain of retail stores with headquarters located in an urban office park in Park Ridge.

What kind of a person was Theodore Crenshaw? Miles searched further, finding biographical data, photos, an account of the man's personal life and professional accomplishments: graduate of Northwestern University; a military stint; former pro wrestler; martial arts expert; married five times.

How in the world did Mr. Zane expected him to go up against such a character? But he was too far in to quit; he would pay Mr. Crenshaw a visit Monday morning.

To Miles, the peaceful-looking suburban corporate campus and plush offices of Marquart Novelties belied the peril that lay within. He parked near the front of the main building at ten minutes before nine, exited his car, and proceeded through two sets of glass doors to a wide atrium and sets of elevators. Upon reaching the top floor executive suites, his attention was drawn to photos which graced the walls of the reception area. They included several of Theodore Crenshaw himself: in a military uniform, as a pro wrestler, and, finally, sitting astride a gleaming black Harley.

The name plate at the receptionist's desk read DOROTHY SCHWARTZ. Behind her desk, double doors and a wall plate reading THEODORE CRENSHAW, CHIEF FINANCIAL OFFICER.

Forcing a smile, he greeted the sullen-faced woman. "Good morning, Ms. Schwartz. I'm here to see Mr. Crenshaw."

Focused on her computer screen, she spoke without looking up. "Do you have an appointment?"

"No. I hoped to catch him at a time when I could have a few minutes."

"Who are you? And whom do you represent?" Still no eye contact.

"Miles Moore, Ma'am, and I am here representing Charles Zane."

"Sorry. It will not be possible for you to see Mr. Crenshaw." She swiveled her chair and began poking through a file drawer, fully turning her back to him.

Being polite wasn't getting him anywhere. "Why isn't it possible? Please answer my question. Is Mr. Crenshaw in his office?"

She spun around and fixed him with a stony look. "Sorry, I've told you. He's not available."

Miles turned away from the desk, but remained, remembering Mr. Zane's explicit instructions: *Do not under any circumstances leave until he gives you the money.* He took a seat.

Schwartz continued to type away, occasionally stopping to take a phone call. Miles noticed that twice she put calls through to Crenshaw. So, the man *was* in his office. How was he to get in there? There had to be a way. What did the heroes in the movies do when faced with such obstacles? There was no use in arguing with Ms. Schwartz, and he couldn't very well barge past her. He would get creative.

Hmm. A minor distraction to get her to leave her station for thirty seconds… Pull the fire alarm? No, too drastic. He looked at his watch. Already nine-ten. Zane had specifically told him around 9 AM. There was no time to lose; he had to come up with something!

Schwartz's phone rang. She answered, and her sullen features took on an alarmed look. "Hold on! I'll be right there!" She slammed the receiver down and bolted out from her desk and down the hall toward the elevators, not caring that Miles was still seated alone in her waiting area.

His chance! Miles walked to Crenshaw's doors and pressed both wide open simultaneously. In front of him was a giant of a man—not at his desk but reclining on a leather sofa, glass of beer in one hand, the other reaching into a dish of cashews on a table in front of him.

"Mr. Crenshaw, my name is Miles Moore, and I am here on behalf of Mr. Charles Zane."

Crenshaw, initially startled at the intrusion, half rose from the couch, leveling a string of curses. "Get out of my office! Whoever you are, you have no business barging in here like this."

Miles didn't move, although his insides were in a tumult. "Mr. Zane sent me here with explicit instructions not to leave until you have handed me the money which you owe him."

"Who? Charles Zane? You're lying! I don't owe Zane anything!" Crenshaw set down his glass and stood. Miles guessed that he must weigh over three hundred pounds and none of it fat.

From somewhere, boldness arose. "No, sir. Mr. Zane doesn't lie to me. I am respectfully asking you to give me what you rightfully owe him." Sure, the brutish Crenshaw could easily tear him apart, but hopefully the weight of Charles Zane's name would be all the protection he needed.

"You need to leave. Now." Crenshaw's initial fit had abated. Apparently, having failed at bullying his unwanted guest, he was changing tactics. "You're trespassing. I could get you in serious trouble. I'll call security." He walked over to his desk and picked up the phone.

"Go ahead. But I'm not leaving without the money. End of discussion." Miles plopped down in a chair and placed both feet squarely on top of the coffee table, rattling the dish of cashews. He recognized that he was dealing with a classic bully; the more Crenshaw raged at him, the more he knew that the man didn't have the upper hand in this confrontation.

Crenshaw stood, phone in hand, cursing under his breath. Then he slammed it back into its cradle. He walked around his desk, sat, pulled out a leather binder full of check blanks, and proceed to write out a check. He slipped it into an envelope, sealed it, and glared at Miles.

"Here, take it!" He held out the envelope.

"Thank you, sir! A pleasure doing business." Miles grabbed the envelope and exited the office. A startled Ms. Schwartz watched him walk past her desk and out the door.

"Congratulations! Looks like you have slain the dragon." Charles Zane beamed, accepting Crenshaw's check. Miles marveled at the transformation of Mr. Zane from the stern, intimidating figure of several days ago into this jovial man.

"Thank you, sir! That encounter was the *grande finale* to a truly novel interview process."

"Well done on your part, even when you didn't always understand."

"Well, your ways became apparent to me the first day I set foot in this place. A fun house mirror, a building block castle in the reception area, and people wearing brightly-colored socks and ties and scarves."

"Exactly. At Toyzania we have fun creating and marketing toys and games and costumes. But make no mistake, that's not what matters most to me. I care more about developing people."

"These last several days have attested to that."

"Glad that it shows. We'll get down to business in a few minutes. But first, you probably have some questions for me about your recent experiences. Fire away!"

"All right, you asked for it. Were you keeping tabs on me throughout each trial? Did you have eyes on me the whole time?"

Zane laughed. "You're not the only person to wonder. I am not omnipresent, but I do keep watch—like Santa Claus. Sometimes from here in my office; sometimes up close and personal in my customers' stores or in their boardrooms; even out on the streets of this city. If not me personally, then one of my elves."

"Hmm. If that's the case, then were you able to make it to your granddaughter's spelling bee? Kassie did very well, by the way."

"Oh, you bet I was there—wouldn't miss it—but invisible most of the time. You see, it was me that grilled that hamburger that you ate for lunch. I hope you enjoyed it."

"Yes, that was probably the best hamburger I have ever eaten in my whole life."

"A wise answer."

"And you have a working relationship with the lady at the costume shop and with Mr. Simmons at the Salvation Army. Correct?"

"Sure. Marcia and Art are trusted coconspirators."

"And Dr. Phillips?"

Zane's head bobbed.

"Last question. How can someone like Theodore Crenshaw hold the job that he has? He didn't look or act like a CFO to me, to put it kindly. In fact, he doesn't even seem to fit in to the corporate world."

"Oh, that's easy to explain. Crenshaw's father, Harvey Crenshaw, owns the company, although he's semi-retired. See, Theodore's a good example of why I work so hard to develop my people. The giant you met the other day is extremely bright and has a lot of potential, but he doesn't care. Never has. Nowadays, poor ol' Harvey spends most of his time cleaning up his son's messes. Congratulations on the way you handled him."

"Were you somehow keeping tabs on me at Crenshaw's office?"

Zane's expression changed. "Admittedly, I went off script with that one. We obviously don't partner with Theodore personally, and I wouldn't normally send an applicant out on an assignment of this nature. So, to answer your question: no. There was no way to monitor that encounter directly. But I took a chance with you and was confident that you would come through, which you did."

"Whew! Thanks! But for a while that morning, I didn't know how things would go. It was by a stroke of luck that I was able to get into his office."

"Is that so? I know from personal experience that Ms. Schwartz, his receptionist, is obstinate and protective of her boss."

"She is, and she wasn't about to let me get past her. But she got some phone call and bolted out of there as if her house were on fire. That gave me the needed break."

"That's odd… Maybe her car alarm suddenly went off in the parking lot. Those things can be very sensitive."

Zane reached into his desk and withdrew a folder. "Now, it's time to get down to the business at hand."

FOUR YEARS LATER

"Hey, Miles. Good game! Your backhand has improved."

"Thanks. But you nailed your serves this time. Right on the line. That's what got me. I couldn't return half of them."

"Maybe so, but I think your issue today was up here." Tony tapped the side of his head. "Your mind is off somewhere else."

Miles reached down into his cooler and pulled out two bottles of water. He and Tony sat across from each other at a shaded picnic table, having finished six sets of tennis. Evenly matched players, they normally split their wins. But today Tony had prevailed in all the sets.

"You're right. My mind has been on something else… actually for quite a while." Miles took a long drink and looked squarely at his friend. "The true meaning of life."

"The true meaning of life, eh? You've been doing some thinking."

"I have. You know, I've always felt that my career was it. Don't get me wrong; my position with Toyzania has truly been satisfying, the fulfillment of my dreams—up until the past several months that is."

"And am I surprised?"

"No. You've told me as much several times."

"Miles, I could see it before you did."

"Yeah, you and my friend, Art, down at the Salvation Army, and a couple of my family members. After the personal challenges I faced this spring, I've finally gotten the message."

"What will you do about it?"

"Oh, I've been formulating a plan, doing my research. I know that I'll have to have a heart-to-heart with Zane this summer about all of this. But that guy has a way of looking right through me. I wouldn't be surprised if he already knows."

Miles lay stretched out on his sofa, his feet hanging over one end. A quiet Sunday night free of any scheduled activities or other social obligations. No sounds other than the hum of the refrigerator. Cellphone and television both turned off. No one else around, and no visitors expected… or wanted.

It felt good to be alone, with time and space to contemplate the upcoming birth of a new stage in life. After weeks of soul-searching and research and the input from trusted friends, he had come to a decision and had laid the groundwork for his next move.

Tomorrow, he would explain it all to Charles Zane.

The door to the office stood wide open. Miles tapped on the frame.

"Come on in. Make yourself at home." Standing in front of his desk, Zane extended his hand toward two chairs and a coffee table, on which sat a frosty pitcher of lemonade, two crystal glasses, and a ceramic jar in the shape of a koala bear. "It's too late in the day for coffee. But never too late for lemonade and cookies."

He filled both glasses, handing one to Miles before taking a seat.

Miles sat and reached toward the cookie jar. "I guess one or two won't spoil my supper." Despite his nervousness over having requested this meeting, he appreciated Mr. Zane's ability to lighten the atmosphere of what might otherwise be an uncomfortable session.

He sipped from his glass and set it down, still searching for a way to begin while admiring the sight of the skyscrapers of Chicago's loop, and Lake Michigan beyond, a view that he had enjoyed from his own office down the hall for nearly four years; in that moment he felt unexpectedly sentimental, thereby finding his opening words.

"As I've said oftentimes before, Toyzania products were a big part of my childhood world. Even in college I began to dream about working here, and I've been able to fulfill that dream." He patted his hand over his heart. "For me, being able to work here and give back has been a joy."

"And..." Zane's eyes were bright, expectant.

"And." Miles fought back tears. "With all due respect for all you've done for me—for what Toyzania means to me—it's time for me to move on."

"Oh?" Zane raised his eyebrows, but otherwise betrayed no surprise.

"What I mean is that I've grown hungry. Hungry for more than anything this job and the current trajectory of my life can ever offer me."

"How so?"

"Please understand that this is not over any sense of dissatisfaction with my position here. Frankly, you have challenged and grown me more than anyone else ever has—right from the start, that day that I stood out on the pier in my court jester costume. This has been an immensely satisfying journey."

"Thank you."

"But now, in large part because of this experience, my eyes have been opened. I've begun to look at everything in life in childlike wonderment, from a new point of view. A magical point of view. An *eternal* point of view."

"Oh, believe it or not, I do understand, and enjoy having had a ringside seat to watch the transformation. I congratulate you."

"Really? You're not upset with me?"

"Upset? No. Sure, you've been a stellar part of our team and will be missed. But remember what I told you when you first started here. I am in the toy business, but also in the business of growing and developing people. Believe it or not, I'm pleased to turn you loose and allow you to do so."

"What a relief! Thank you for understanding."

"So, what's next? Where do you go from here?"

"That's the scary part. Leaving this familiar world and stepping out into a new one. For me, that begins with fulltime seminary this fall."

"Aah!" Zane beamed.

"For the past several months I've been having dreams—literally dreaming vivid dreams while asleep—of standing in front of a huge crowd of people, teaching them how to have what I have, in heart, mind, and soul. I want them all to be transformed."

"Then, Miles, I wish you Godspeed. You've been called, and you must go forth. It would be wrong not to do so."

Matthew 5:6 (KJV)
Blessed are they which do hunger and thirst after righteousness: for they shall be filled.

Matthew 5:6 (AMP)
Blessed [joyful, nourished by God's goodness] are those who hunger and thirst for righteousness [those who actively seek right standing with God], for they will be [completely] satisfied.

Matthew 5:6 (MSG)
You're blessed when you've worked up a good appetite for God. He's food and drink in the best meal you'll ever eat.

JONATHAN

The Jaguar glided through the parking lot of Statler's Supermarket, its engine purring.

"Look at that masterpiece, Ted. What I wouldn't give for a chance to hot-wire it. Race up and down Highway 12 a few times before he even comes out of the store. I've heard that thing will do over a hundred-and-twenty, easy."

Alex and Ted, sitting in Ted's pickup truck, watched the vintage sports car pull into a spot at the front of the building. A young man climbed out and walked into the store. Jonathan Wright, Alex's cousin.

Ted rapped the steering wheel. "I agree that it's a beautiful car. But here you go again. I'm getting sick of listening to you talk that way."

"Hey, buddy. Don't give me that attitude. You're not above coveting other people's stuff either."

"True. But I know the difference between a little jealousy and being obsessed. You scare me at times, the way you talk. I almost believe you would pull such a stunt."

"What, me steal Jonathan's car? No way. But that doesn't mean that I can't think about it. Let's face it. Jonathan gets all the breaks in life. I can't imagine any greater satisfaction than that of seeing the guy take a hit once in a while."

"And that's what scares me." Ted started the truck. "We're getting out of here before you get any more ideas."

He put it in gear and sped out of the parking lot. "When you start in this way, I know enough to shut it down. Therefore, I'm running you home. Maybe your wife can talk some sense into you before you say or do something stupid in front of a bunch of your family members this weekend."

"Oh, she'd probably try… if I ever bothered to tell her."

"Jonathan has arrived!"

Three heads pivoted toward the sound of the summons from the front door.

"Hey, good talking with you, Alex." A clap on the shoulder. "We'll catch up with you later."

The trio of uncles turned and trooped off to where a young man and woman stood in the foyer. Alex watched them join others moving toward the couple.

Sure… don't mind me. Far be it from me to interfere with Jonathan's day. This was turning out to be just another typical family event, with Jonathan as the main attraction. Now, a fiancée in the mix, drawing even more attention and intrigue.

The unintended but frequent slights of otherwise well-meaning family members and friends stung, even now evidenced by overheard comments to the young couple.

"You'll be a great pastor."

"Thank you. I'm doing the best I can. The rest is up to the Lord."

"Glad for you. We always knew that you would be the family's shining star."

"Oh, no. I'm hardly that."

"And how about that portfolio! You continue to beat the market. You're savvy enough to be an analyst."

"Thank you, but my heart is in what I'm doing, trying to get through school so that I can better serve the Lord. I wouldn't be satisfied doing anything else."

After a few minutes Jonathan looked up and, spotting Alex, excused himself from the group. Naturally. Jonathan was always nice to him. *Genuinely* nice. Gracious, kind, and humble.

"Good to see you, Alex. Is your beautiful family here today?"

"Yes."

"So glad you all could make it. I miss our talks and the time we used to be able to spend together. I'm afraid we're both caught up in the new paces of our lives."

"I understand," Alex responded mechanically, privately seething. Jonathan couldn't be so polite and happy all the time; there had to be a chink in his armor that he could exploit to show the world that the family's favorite wasn't everything they thought he was.

And—as of the past few days—an idea had been taking shape.

"Honey, I've got to run out tonight." Alex gave Samantha a quick kiss.

"That's fine. Is everything okay?"

"Yeah. I just need to check on a couple of things at the Club. The new cook is manning the grill by himself tonight, and he's still learning." A blatant lie.

"All right. Try not to be too late. You promised to read to the kids before their bedtime."

Most Monday evenings Alex spent at home, leaving his assistant in charge of the kitchen. But tonight, there were other plans. He backed his brand-new 2003 Honda Civic out of the garage and drove into town, but in the opposite direction of Club 26.

"Ted, can you get me into Jonathan's garage?"

"Alex! You know how I feel about this."

"How about for a hundred bucks? Cash."

"A hundred bucks? You serious? When?"

"Right now. You'd better believe I'm serious. I may not be able to steal his car, but that doesn't mean I can't do something else—something we can do with without getting caught, I promise."

"Okay…" Ted hesitated. "This is stupid, and I should know better. But for that kind of money, I'll help you. But I won't do anything beyond unlocking the door."

They headed to the outskirts of the city in Ted's truck. Jonathan's house fronted a winding blacktop road. In the darkness, the faint silhouettes of a line of dwellings mingled with those of pine trees appeared on the horizon. Ted pulled to the curb in front of an undeveloped lot well short of their target, and the two men stepped out. Jonathan's house appeared deserted except for faint light seeping through blinds in the back. The Chosen One would be back in his family room, probably with his nose in a textbook or his computer, oblivious to anything else going on around him. This would be a simple job.

Ted, with gloved hands, expertly withdrew a set of instruments from a small leather case, and within thirty seconds had opened the side door into the garage.

"Okay, get back in your truck. I'll be out in a jif." Alex pulled a flashlight from his rain jacket. He slipped inside and gazed admiringly at the vintage sports car, a 1951 Jaguar XK 120C, the prize that Jonathan had acquired for a song at auction two years earlier.

Keeping his flashlight aimed at the floor and pulling a small file from his pocket, he proceeded to carve a series of long lines and swirls into the satiny silver finish along the full passenger side of the car. Then exited the garage and pulled the door shut, making sure it was locked before rejoining Ted back outside. No one would ever know he had entered.

"Oh! What happened here?" Jonathan slapped a palm to his forehead in the student parking lot, for the first time noticing deep scratches in the passenger side finish. He ran his finger over the jagged edges where paint had been scraped away and the underlying metal scarred.

Dismay turned to anger. This was too-well executed to have been caused by a tree branch or a careless person. This was deliberate! When had this happened? His parking spot should have been safe, in full view of the student center. There had never been an issue before.

That evening Jonathan shared his frustration with two of his classmates during a study session in his living room. "I've never had anything like this happen before. Must have been at either the gas station or the grocery store yesterday. But *why?* Why would someone do this? Have I done something to offend someone?"

"Sorry, buddy, you may never know. But if you want, I'll talk to my uncle that has a body shop over by school. He does good work and will give you a fair price."

"Thanks! I may take you up on that. Anyway, it's just a car and can be fixed. I'll just have to get over it."

"Order up!" Alex called out to a waiter, setting two platters of prime rib on the counter. Friday night was Club 26's busiest, and the dining room was packed with customers, with a half-dozen or so more waiting at the front door. On such nights, he would generally roll up his sleeves and pitch in wherever needed in the kitchen. Tonight, the front line.

But even with the pressures of the evening's rush he felt lighter, almost jubilant. By now the fruits of his work would have been discovered. Score one for his side! The weekend was coming—the family's annual Fourth of July gathering at Jonathan's house—and with it the opportunity to witness Jonathan's reaction first-hand.

Alex guzzled sodas and stuffed chili dogs into his mouth, alert for any reference to the escapade of a few days ago. But Jonathan seemed happy and relaxed, moving among the several guests on his patio, and fiancée Candace looked to be enjoying her share of attention and compliments as well.

"Hey, when are you two getting married?"

"After we both get done with school." Jonathan put his arm around Candace and gave her a peck on the cheek.

"Jonathan's promised me the honeymoon of my dreams," she chirped. "I couldn't have found a better looking, intelligent and talented man. And, he drives a vintage Jaguar."

Jonathan blushed.

"Two more years at the University for me," she added. "In fact, I'll need to leave soon. I've got a long drive back to school yet today, and a paper due on Monday."

"Jonathan, speaking of your Jaguar, how's it running?"

"Smooth as ever. Want to take a look at her?"

"Yes!" A group of men trooped off toward the garage, and Alex jumped up to join them. This was it!

Jonathan unlocked the back door and flipped a switch. The garage was bathed in light and an admiring group crowded inside. Alex casually strolled around the full perimeter of the car, looking to admire his handiwork. But, alas, the finish appeared perfect! Not a scratch to be seen.

"That is truly a work of art!" exclaimed an uncle. "Do you still drive it to school every day?"

"Yes, absolutely. For now, it's my only vehicle, and there's no use my having it if it's going to be locked up in my garage all the time."

Alex quietly seethed. Nothing wrong! How?

"Who wants to go for a spin?"

A hand went up, and within a minute Jonathan and an excited passenger zipped out of the driveway and down the street. Alex watched until the car was out of sight, then returned to the back yard.

Samantha found him sitting alone. "Alex, are you okay? You've barely said a word for the past hour."

"I'm fine, Dear. Got a lot on my mind."

Yeah, like justice!

While other celebrants talked and ate, he brooded. Once again Jonathan had scored. What would it take to break through that annoying façade of happiness and contentment? There had to be some way to get his goat, to provoke him to anger. What was his vulnerable spot?

"Tell me, Ted." Alex flung his line out into the stream. "You've known Jonathan for years. How does he make *you* feel?"

The two stood on a riverbank. Alex found the tranquility of his private fishing spot a welcomed respite from the pressures of work and home and would often meet Ted there.

"That guy certainly has it together. Must admit that I envy him at times. Nothing ever seems to rattle him. Always in a good mood, smiling and friendly, and gets lots of attention."

"That's what gets to me. We're first cousins, about the same age and grew up together. We used to be treated equally by everyone. Not anymore. He's clearly become everyone's favorite."

"Well, Alex. You'll just have to accept the fact that life's not fair."

"No, it's not—in my case with Jonathan being the one who gets all the breaks in life, the one with the good looks, the friends, the athletic ability, the girl…"

"Don't forget the car," Ted interrupted.

"Right. The Jaguar, and the smarts to make it in grad school and beat the stock market. The guy gets everything."

"You're right. Some people are simply dealt a better hand than the rest of us. Those are the ones you see out playing golf at their country clubs or lounging around their backyard swimming pools."

"But life can't be fair all the time for everyone, not even for Jonathan. And—as of this morning—I may have come up with an idea to even things up."

"Watch yourself." Ted tugged his pole gently, feeling a nibble. "The guy's all about God. You don't want to mess with God. In other words, you're playing with fire. Please take my advice and let it go."

"Let it go? No way. I may have found a way to rattle him, maybe even instill fear. You still got mice in your barn?"

"I do, but I'm not getting involved this time."

"Not even for another hundred bucks?"

"What if he gets home early? Then we're toast."

"Chill out, Ted. It's Wednesday. Jonathan will be at school all day."

Alex's and Ted's journey had this time been in a borrowed van. To anyone who happened to pay attention, the vehicle standing in Jonathan's driveway would be considered that of a repairman or delivery man.

Utilizing his miniature tool kit, Ted easily opened the same door into the garage.

"You stay out here and keep watch. I'll be out in a minute or two." Alex proceeded through the garage and straight into the kitchen, carrying a small cardboard box. From it he lifted out a paper bag filled with gray forms—dead mice, nearly two dozen of the stiffening little bodies.

Moving about the kitchen and wearing gloves, he deposited mice carcasses into unseen places—behind the refrigerator, into lower cupboards, below the sink, and at the back of the pantry. Jonathan wouldn't be so self-assured, fearing that his house had been infested.

As Alex finished his task, Ted leaned in through the doorway behind him, shaking his head. "Let's move it. We gotta get out of here. The neighbors will begin coming home soon."

"Oh, don't worry." He picked up the box and looked about the kitchen for any evidence of their having been there. "See, I've pushed one of Jonathan's buttons where it hurts, but there's no real harm done. Let's be on our way."

Less than ten minutes after the van had pulled into the Wright driveway, it was gone.

Jonathan leaned forward to inspect the evidence. "I don't know what to say," he muttered to the uniformed technician.

"Sorry this happened, Jonathan, but you're safe—at least from rodent infestation or poison." The technician prodded the carcass of one of the dead mice with a pair of tweezers. "There is a concern over what our lab has found, but not for the reason that you might suspect."

"Oh? What would that reason be? I keep my home spotless and have never had an issue like this before. Never."

Upon his disturbing find at home the evening before, Jonathan had contacted a local pest control firm to have his home inspected. Today's follow-up visit was at the firm's local lab facility.

"That's my point." The tech scratched his head, a puzzled and troubled look on his face. "I believe you. That's why our findings lead me to believe that this was some twisted idea of a prank. All twenty-two of these mice died from ingesting Bromethalin, a common rat poison. And our inspectors found no traces of that substance anywhere in your home."

"No, there couldn't be. I have no reason to keep any of that around."

"What I'm telling you is that those mice were dead before they were placed there."

"Whoa! Someone planted them? Already dead?"

"Yes. Long story short, you don't have an infestation issue here. You might, however, consider contacting the police. In my opinion, this could be considered a criminal act, someone entering your locked home and leaving this."

"Wow! Why would someone want to attack me this way?"

"Who knows? But, if I were you, I'd be trying my best to identify anyone that could be an enemy, or at least holding a grudge."

Jonathan cringed involuntarily at the name that immediately popped into his mind.

Jonathan's cell phone buzzed. He leaned back from his studies and picked it up.

"Hey, son, we're back home."

"Hey, thanks for calling, Dad. Did you and Mom finally decide on wallpaper for your bedroom?"

"We did, but it was an ordeal. I had no idea of how many varieties of wallpaper are available. Now your mother and sister are talking about ceiling border. Can you believe it?"

Jonathan laughed. "I wish you all well with that."

"How about you? How'd your visit with the pest control folks go?"

"Oh, quite interesting. Good news and bad news."

"Okay. Give me the good news."

"There is no infestation problem. And no toxins in the house."

"Whew! That's a relief. What's the bad news?"

"The mice were planted here by some person or persons. A cruel prank, technically a crime. They were poisoned before being brought in."

"Ooh! And who might the culprit be?"

"Dad, I've given that a lot of thought, and, sad to say, there is one individual that comes to mind. I'll have to verify that, and then decide what to do about it."

"Well, let justice be accomplished. But don't do anything drastic."

"To be honest with you, less than honorable thoughts have crossed my mind. But don't worry. I will try to handle this in the right way. Wisdom and discretion will prevail."

Ted smirked. "Dude, you've struck out twice. Give it up!" He stuck up his hand. "Hey, a couple more beers please."

Alex glared. "Shut your mouth! What right do you have to tell me what to do?" He slapped the tabletop, nearly toppling two beer bottles. Heads turned from nearby tables at the commotion.

Ted recoiled, wary of the expression on his friend's face. "Sorry."

"Listen, Ted, the comparisons and humiliation have gone on for years. 'Jonathan is this.' 'Jonathan did that.' 'Jonathan, Jonathan, Jonathan.' And what do I get? 'Alex, how did you manage to land such a sweet wife and children.'"

He slapped the table again. "You have no idea what it's like to live in someone else's shadow. To be constantly compared, and always falling short. No matter what… it never measures up to Jonathan."

Ted guzzled the last of his beer. "Dude, you're scaring me, becoming obsessed. Get over it. Jonathan's a decent guy… and he doesn't even care."

Conversation paused while the waitress set two more bottles on the table.

Alex rubbed his hands across his face. "That's my point. He doesn't care. He doesn't even seem to notice. I asked him the other day about how things were going, and there was no mention of the mice! The jerk is unflappable. That's what makes me so mad!"

"Look. Forget about Jonathan. You've got a wife, two children, a house that's paid for, a good job, and—if you don't blow it—a good reputation. Please, leave the guy alone."

Alex sat lost in thought. Then his face lit up. "Reputation! You said, 'reputation.' That's the ticket! Jonathan has always been squeaky clean. Everyone thinks he's a saint. That's his vulnerable spot. Thanks, Ted. Great idea."

Ted groaned. "Whoa! That wasn't supposed to be a suggestion. Remember that you're dealing with someone who's going into the ministry. You might make God Himself mad."

"Ted, are you wimping out on me?"

"You know me. I enjoy a good caper, but you're talking about attacking Jonathan's character. That's taking things to a new level. Off limits as far as I'm concerned."

"Not for me. And, Ted, I know you. Regardless of how you feel about it, you'll go along with me if there's enough money in it."

"Maybe so, but my price goes up for something like this. At least triple."

Alex stopped talking, eyes fixed absently on his hands, which were idly folding a paper napkin into smaller and smaller squares. At last, he raised his head. "Ted, is Susie still working at the store?"

"Yeah, long hours. Has it rough. Her jerk of a husband walked out and left her and the kids high and dry." Ted looked wary. "Why are you asking about her?"

"Think back to when we were all in high school. She was known for being willing to take a walk on the wild side, to try about anything. If she would agree to my little proposal and could use some extra cash, I've got a proposition. Do you think she's up to it?"

"She's probably desperate, but also trying to leave her old life behind. Don't expect her to be like she was in high school."

"I'm not asking her to go all the way through with anything, but to merely create a scene. Can you give her a call?"

"Are you sure about this? You're moving into the danger zone, talking about trying to destroy your cousin in a very personal way, this time asking someone else to get involved. Someone besides me."

"Perhaps, but my mind is made up. Finally, an idea that will work. Are you on board or not? Remember, there's money in it for you and for Susie."

"Maybe, but like I told you, my rate goes up. Three-hundred dollars for me, and at least that much for her."

"Okay, not a problem."

Ted recoiled. "Stop! Buddy, don't you understand sarcasm? Six-hundred dollars? I was kidding about the money. What you're not understanding is that Susie can't afford to pull something like this. She's got kids and is trying to get her life back on track."

"Oh yeah?" Alex reached into his pocket and pulled out a wad of currency. "See, money is not an issue." He peeled back several bills, all of them hundreds. "I meant what I said."

"But you're talking about your hard-earned dough. Is this worth all that?"

"Yes, Ted. To me it is. Unless you've been in my shoes, you can't understand. I've got the money and am determined to make this happen. Are you with me or not?"

Ted sat for a long time. "For the record, this is a dumb idea, and you can't afford it, but…okay, I'll talk with Susie. She and I both need the money."

"I was right—although I wish I wasn't," Jonathan murmured. "The culprit has conclusively been identified, having both motive and means. I was able to confirm my suspicions this morning."

He looked across the top of a large pizza at two friends. The three had finished a long study session in the school library and stopped at a local eatery for a late-night meal.

"We're talking about your cousin Alex, right?"

"Yes, unfortunately. I should have seen it right away, but I guess I didn't want to."

"So we know that he's the guilty party. What do you plan to do about it, future Pastor Wright, exact revenge?"

"In a sense—yes."

"Jonathan!"

"Hold on!" Jonathan held up both hands. "Let me explain." He glanced upward and then back to his friends. "God, please forgive me, but I've got a plan. No harm to Alex of course, but something that will cause him to think about what he's doing. Kind of like holding a mirror up to him. All in lovingkindness."

"And what might that be? An eye for an eye?"

Jonathan shook his head. "Yes… and no. Have you ever heard of counting coup?"

"What?"

"Counting coup. A tactic used by some tribes of American Indians during their wars as an act of bravery, to intimidate their enemies. Basically, a warrior would sneak up on his unsuspecting foe and touch him with a coup stick. This let the enemy know that he could have been killed, but instead was spared. A type of psychological warfare."

"Oh. Like what King David did to Saul when Saul was pursuing him. Snuck up in the dark and sliced a piece from Saul's cloak, thereby demonstrating mercy when he easily could have slain him."

"Exactly! I want to help Alex understand what he's been doing to me from *my* point of view, but privately, in a merciful way, without humiliating or otherwise hurting him. It's time that I counted coup."

"Whew! This could get interesting. What have you got in mind?"

Early Friday morning Alex flipped on the bright overhead lights and stepped into his kitchen, performing the routine tasks of getting his workspace ready for what would likely be a busy day; grills and ovens fired up and a last-minute check of the produce drawers to be sure that everything was in stock. Last stop was the walk-in cooler. He tugged on the handle and the heavy door swung open. To the left several wrapped packages of ground beef, steaks, and pork chops… and a plain brown paper bag. What was that? He pulled the bag open and peered into the top. Five little frozen forms lay nestled within. Five dead mice!

How in the world…? He staggered backward and involuntarily pitched the bag so that it spilled its grisly contents across the floor.

He scrambled out of the cooler and returned with a pair of gloves and another bag. Bent down and began to gingerly pick up the carcasses—then stopped. These were *toy* mice. Made of fabric. In disgust, he scooped all of them into his bag.

Then realization struck. Jonathan was on to him!

Battling fear and anger over this unexpected change in the field of play, Alex somehow managed a full day of serving a seeming record number of hungry customers. Upon finally locking the front doors for the night, he looked at his watch. Nearly midnight! What a day this had been! With an aching back and thoughts in turmoil, he couldn't wait to get home to soak in a steaming hot tub before falling into bed.

"Good night!" he called to his equally tired assistant. "I'm heading home. See you tomorrow." He shucked off his apron and tossed it into a laundry hamper.

"Good night. Try to get some rest. You look like you need it."

Crossing the gravel parking space from the back door of Club 26 to the Honda, Alex admired its gleaming finish in the glow of the security lighting. But there was something else; along the driver side of the vehicle were a series of long, curving scratches.

"What? Not this!" He lurched forward and ran his finger along the deepest scratch…except that it wasn't a scratch. "Huh? Crayon marks?" The waxy substance easily rubbed off under his finger. Relieved, he unlocked the door and climbed into the car, his thoughts and emotions spinning out of control.

That jerk got me again. But not the next time! Then it won't matter. It will be too late for him. The damage will have already been done.

Three evenings later Alex felt encouraged. Ted seemed to have finally warmed to the idea of staging a frame up.

"Hey, Buddy." Ted spoke through the opened window of his pickup truck, where Alex had walked up to him after closing up the Club for the evening. "I've talked with Susie about your plan like you asked. All that's left is getting Jonathan over to her house tomorrow night, and she'll take things from there."

"Thanks. All according to my instructions, right?"

"Yep. It's a go. The hard part will be your convincing Jonathan to go over there. You'll have to come up with something creative."

"No problem. I've got an idea." Alex tapped the side of his head. "Remember, Jonathan tends to be too nice for his own good. And he's naïve—especially when it comes to women. He would never forego an opportunity to reach out to some poor soul in need, even if it's little more than dropping off a few bags of groceries for a single mother on a tight budget. And I found out that his schedule is open tomorrow night, any time after seven o'clock."

"Good. Susie should be home from work by then. Plenty of time to change her clothes, fix her hair and put on her makeup, and get her kids out of the house."

"Have her call Jonathan early tomorrow morning and ask him for help with some grocery money, at least some milk and eggs. He would be aware of how she's been struggling to get her life back on track after her husband bailed out. He'll fall right into the trap."

"Sounds like a plan."

"And tell her she's got exactly ten minutes to get him into some compromising position in her front room."

"Good enough." Ted nodded. "How about me? What will my role be in all of this?"

"Your part will be done, so steer clear. I, on the other hand, will be close at hand and will go to the front door exactly ten minutes after Jonathan goes inside. I'll be carrying my camera. This will be fun!"

Alex hunched down in the driver seat of the Honda, across the street and well down the block from Susie's home. Darkness was falling, and her porch light was lit. But no signs of activity.

The digital clock on the dash read eight-o-five.

Earlier in the day, Ted had called him at the Club to assure him that Susie had indeed placed her call of distress to Jonathan. The kindhearted and gullible man would stop by in the evening to bring her some desperately needed grocery items.

The glow of a set of headlights appeared from behind, and Alex hunkered down further.

Seconds later the Jaguar purred past and pulled to the curb several car-lengths ahead. Alex watched Jonathan step from the car and stride across the street, several plastic grocery bags dangling from his hands. He reached the front door and pressed the doorbell.

Peering through binoculars, Alex watched the inside door swing open. Susie's petite form was silhouetted by the bright living room lights behind her. She held the glass storm door wide, beckoning Jonathan to enter. The storm door closed, and the figures disappeared inside.

Okay, now things should get interesting! He looked at the clock. Eight-o-seven. Jonathan had wound up being his usual prompt self, and everything was going according to plan.

The minutes seemed to crawl. At eight-fifteen he set down the binoculars and grabbed his camera.

He climbed out of the car and crossed the street at an angle toward Susie's house. This would work even better than expected. The full-glass storm door and the inside door still standing wide open might even allow for some incriminating photos taken from outside, unseen. Excitedly, he rechecked his camera settings and placed his index finger on the button, prepared to witness and photograph a scandal.

But when he reached the front step, a figure appeared behind the storm door, and it swung open wide. Susie stood there by herself, smiling, and extending a hand of welcome. "Hi, Alex. Come on in."

What?

Heart sinking, he stepped in and looked around the front room—to behold both Jonathan and Samantha, comfortably seated with soft drinks in hand!

Susie remained at the front door, calling out, "Hey kids, time to go!" From somewhere came the sounds of running feet.

She turned to look at her guests. "Take all the time you need. The kids and I will be over at my sister's place tonight. And Jonathan…" —she smiled gratefully— "thank you for the groceries. Payday isn't until next week, and we were running short."

With that, Susie and her kids paraded past Alex and disappeared out the front door. Jonathan stood to close the door behind them before turning back to face Alex. "Believe it or not, I am not enjoying this."

He sat back down. Samantha remained seated without speaking, her hands clutched in her lap.

Alex paced back and forth in front of them, battling a flood of emotions: anger, embarrassment, self-pity, and a grim acceptance of his circumstances. He could think of nothing to say but glared at the floor.

"Alex," Jonathan said. "Let's stop all of this business. I have no issue with you, and no interest in sparring with you."

"Of course, you don't. I'm not worth the effort," he replied. The Chosen One had not been provoked after all and had instead wound up being the Good Samaritan in the exchange. That was how things *always* went for Jonathan.

"Please. We're family, not competitors. We've grown up together, and that's important to me." Jonathan raised both arms in a posture of surrender. "I want us to get along."

"In other words, what I've been trying to do to you doesn't matter." Alex moaned, turning around to look at his wife. Samantha remained still but was trembling. What was that look in her eyes? Pity? Shame? Maybe fear? By all appearances, he had hurt her far more than he had bothered his cousin.

For the first time feeling some remorse, he turned back to Jonathan. "Okay, I admit it. You've outmaneuvered me. How did you know it was me?"

"Alex, you're not as subtle or sneaky as you think. When I learned that the dead mice in my house had been poisoned with Bromethalin, I simply stopped in at the hardware store where you typically shop. Mr. Thomas told me that you had just been in and bought some of the stuff."

"Okay, so you got me. You could have had me criminally charged. Why didn't you finish me off?"

"I have no interest in prosecuting you or otherwise hurting you."

"No?"

Jonathan continued. "It's called mercy. If anyone knows about mercy, it's me, Jonathan Wright. You yourself have said that I get all the breaks in life. Well, I do agree that I've been given more than I deserve."

"You do have it made."

"You've heard the expression, 'you reap what you sow.'"

"Sure, let me have it, Preacher."

"Alex, I'm referring to myself, not you. I've been granted mercy in life in countless instances because I do my best to extend mercy. Believe it or not, you're not the first one to try to trip me up. Others have tried, and those situations have required effort in achieving resolution and reconciliation. That's all I want for us."

"Have all of those others gotten fake mice and crayon marks? Set up and made fools of in front of other people?" He glanced back at Samantha.

Jonathan stifled a chuckle. "No. My intent was never to humiliate you, but to keep this private. I am sorry that it had to turn out this way. Your situation required more creativity, a lesson in knowing what it feels like to be on the receiving end of an attack, all without causing any real harm."

"With you coming out looking like the one who's got it all together."

"I'm far from that. Rather, I'm still a work in progress. Trust me, when I discovered that my Jaguar had been keyed, my first thoughts were all about revenge, payback."

"Revenge? You?"

"But that doesn't work. Let's face it, I'm going into the ministry. Further attacks, and persecution, and other kinds of trials are guaranteed to come my way. Perhaps I should be thanking you for giving me a practice run."

A soft knock sounded at the front door, and Ted poked his head in. "Is it safe to enter?"

Alex jerked his head around. "Ted, what're you doing here?" First his own wife, then Susie and her kids—and now his best friend.

Jonathan got up from his chair and offered a salute. "Speaking of mercy, here's my most recent angel of mercy. Good evening, Ted."

"Who, me?" Ted looked surprised but pleased at the words.

"Yes," Jonathan continued. "Ted granted me mercy in a big way this evening."

Alex shook his head. This couldn't be. "Ted? Merciful?"

"Yes. It's funny how it all goes around. Ted first favored me—really both of us, if you think about it—by tipping me off as to what was supposed to happen tonight. In turn, I can offer mercy and complete forgiveness to you. For your information, Ted was not even supposed to be involved tonight, and had no reason to intervene in tonight's little gathering, but he chose to be here."

Ted, recovering from his surprise, looked pleased with himself. "At your service."

Ignoring Jonathan, Alex scowled at Ted. "What happened tonight? It was not supposed to go down this way."

Ted looked about nervously and moved toward the front door. "Sorry to have double-crossed you, but it was because of the way you talked and behaved when we first discussed this plan."

"Oh, and how did I talk and behave?"

"Truthfully, you scared me. You were angry and bent on attacking Jonathan's character and reputation in a manner that has been eating at me. He's going into the ministry. I'll admit that my decisions and actions in life haven't always been on the straight and narrow, but I know better than to cross that line."

"So, you arranged for an audience." Alex again looked at his wife, who continued to watch without moving or speaking.

"Not an audience… but witnesses," Ted corrected. "I needed Samantha to be here, and I wanted to be close by myself. We didn't know how you would react once you realized you'd been set up, and we were concerned for both Susie's and Jonathan's sakes."

"Sorry, but I don't buy your self-righteous, merciful attitude. I don't care what Jonathan said about you. You're in this for the money. That makes you guilty. But you lose this time. You won't get a dime after pulling this on me."

Jonathan spoke up. "Hold on a minute. Ted, explain to Alex what you did."

"You're right about the guilty thing with me, Alex. I can't argue with that," Ted said. "Except that in this case I had a change of heart.

Made the call to Jonathan and changed the game, knowing full-well that it would cost me three-hundred dollars to do so."

For once, Alex had no retort. "So, you're not worried about getting paid?"

"Nope. Not this time."

Alex was stunned. What had happened to his friend? "So, how did our plan get turned upside-down, with all of you turning on me?"

"Let me explain," Jonathan said. "Ted first called me to tip me off about your plans. Then the four of us talked. Ted, Samantha, Susie, and me. Together, we worked out a new arrangement."

"A new arrangement?"

"Yes, and you watched it play out flawlessly tonight." Jonathan counted off on his fingers. "First, thanks to Ted, I was protected from what could have been an awkward and damaging situation; in turn, I forgive both you and Ted for the roles you played in the car-keying and dead mice capers; third, Suzie and her kids are provided with some much-needed groceries; fourth, you are spared from making a critical and foolish mistake; and, finally, your poor wife learns why you've been struggling lately. Everyone wins!"

Matthew 5:7 (KJV)
Blessed are the merciful: for they shall obtain mercy.

Matthew 5:7 (AMP)
Blessed [content, sheltered by God's promises] are the merciful, for they will receive mercy.

Matthew 5:7 (MSG)
You're blessed when you care. At the moment of being 'care-full,' you find yourselves cared for.

CALVIN

The 18-wheeler pulled on to the highway, turning south. Calvin Sidney stood and watched until it had disappeared into the night, the growl of its engine gradually giving way to sounds of crickets and frogs. There must be a pond somewhere nearby. Nature's chorus and the odors of the warm June night felt soothing. He breathed in the sweet air.

Relief had come none too soon.

Pete, the congenial trucker, had been good company at first, jovial and talkative about his life on the road and all the interesting parts of the country that he had seen. Too bad, Calvin thought, that such a sociable creature should have to spend so much of his life alone in the cab of a truck. No wonder he was willing to allow a total stranger to be his traveling companion for what would have been an overnight road trip.

But the initially smooth journey became an ordeal. Two un-scheduled stops, first for refueling, and again when a warning light appeared on the truck's instrument panel, making Pete nervous enough to stop and raise the hood. He corrected the issue, and everything worked fine after that. But time had been lost. What if the truck had broken down altogether?

Then Pete had begun to ask questions. Calvin kept his responses brief and vague and feigned sleepiness, hoping the guy would let up. But the less information he offered, the more the driver wanted to know. What difference could it make where Calvin was from, or where he was going, or what line of work he was in? Why did Pete need to know where he had grown up and if he had any family?

By then midnight had passed. Calvin was tired, and his patience was wearing thin under the onslaught. More critically, he knew that in his physically worn state his well-polished art of masquerade wouldn't be at its best. He would have to lose Pete and find another ride. It didn't matter where they were. He would find another means of transportation, even in the middle of the night.

The welcome sight of an all-night truck stop came into view.

"I'll need to get off here."

"Buddy, I can drop you off, but you're out in the middle of nowhere." Obvious disappointment showed on Pete's round face.

"That's fine. I want to stop here. I'm hungry and I gotta use the can." Calvin spit the last words out; there would be no argument.

Pete downshifted and pulled off the highway and onto the outer perimeter of a graveled parking area. Even before the truck came to a complete stop, Calvin had pushed open the door.

Pete looked at his passenger longingly. "I'll wait if you want."

"No, that's okay. Go on. I need to stretch my legs. I may hang out here." Calvin hefted his pack from the floor between his feet.

"Okay, have it your way. But there's nothing here. You'll be thumbing for another ride after you've gotten something to eat."

"That's all right. Thank you for the lift." He hopped down from the cab, offering a friendly wave before slamming the door shut. With a clank of shifting gears and the revving of the engine, the diesel moved on.

The semi and its nosy driver gone, Calvin turned his attention to his immediate physical needs. There would be a men's room and plenty of food options inside. And maybe a map. He was somewhere in northern Ohio—or was it Indiana? —on a secondary highway, far from any city or town. It didn't matter. He knew to keep traveling due south to where, eventually, he would reach his friend, one of the few he still trusted.

He shifted the strap of his backpack on his shoulder. Stuffed inside were his crumpled up white dress shirt, suit jacket, trousers, and tie. And a binder containing critical legal documents. Hours earlier, at the beginning of his journey, he had used a cramped and grimy service station men's room in suburban Lansing to change from his fine business attire into the T-shirt, jeans, and baseball cap he now wore.

Now to use the store's bathroom, find something to take the edge off of hunger, and get back on the road. The windowed facade of the building featured several neon beer logos and colorful state lottery signage and revealed that the place was essentially unoccupied. There were no vehicles at the pumps and no sign of customer traffic anywhere outside. Inside the front doors, a bored-looking attendant with a spiked hairdo and ear buds fiddled with some electronic game behind the cashier stand. There were likely others somewhere on the premises; three cars were parked along the building's north side, and a remote outpost like this wouldn't be left in the care of only one employee.

Calvin pushed open the front doors and headed straight toward the back, unacknowledged by the cashier who was still engrossed in his game.

The short hallway to the restrooms passed by the open doorway of a break room. There a second individual sat at a table, his back to the door. He was sipping from a small shiny flask and watching the rebroadcast of some talk show on television. This man, somewhat older and neatly dressed, would be a manager. Either allowed to drink on the job, or else he didn't care about rules this time of night. Okay, there were at least two men on site. Neither of them paying him any notice.

Returning from the men's room to the main part of the store, Calvin looked around. No other employees or customers in sight and no cars at the pumps outside. He lingered among the aisles and picked up a wrapped turkey sandwich, a bag of chips, and a drink. How could an establishment like this afford to stay open all night? Obviously, a rural area; nothing but farmland for the past thirty or forty miles. Very little traffic on the highway, and none had gone by for the past several minutes.

He looked over at the cashier, still distracted, and thought about the second individual in the back, watching TV and drinking. The display cases of snack foods and other items needed restocking. Calvin understood the business enough to know that the profit margin on fuel sales was slim, and establishments like this depended on convenience store sales to remain profitable. How could the business owner be making any money? Perhaps there were other kinds of commerce being conducted here—an entirely plausible explanation. If that was the case, he should get on his way sooner rather than later. He had no desire to be around any situation that smelled of criminal activity.

Calvin pulled his cap down low on his forehead. "Must be boring working the night shift." He offered a friendly smile to the young cashier, who he could see wore a black T-shirt with skull and crossbones on the front.

"Huh?" The cashier pulled out his earbuds.

"Quiet here tonight. Must be boring for you."

"Yep, it is. But at least I don't have to do much; hardly anyone comes around this late."

"I guess that's true. Hey, do you sell road maps? And, if so, can you show me where we're located?"

The kid scowled and slapped down his game. "You've interrupted me when I was about to beat my best score." After poking around behind the counter, he produced one, unfolded it, and pointed. "You're right here."

"Hey, thanks!" Calvin gathered up the food items and the map and placed some money on the counter. "Keep the change."

No response.

"Hey, by the way, is the fishing up north of here, in Michigan, any good this time of year?"

"I dunno. I don't fish." He stuck the buds back into his ears and turned his attention back to his game.

"Okay, thanks anyway." Calvin doubted the kid even heard him.

Back outside, Calvin walked around the end of the building, out of view of the front windows, and found a bench on which to sit and eat. He studied the three vehicles parked at the curb in front of him. The Ford Taurus, probably a 2000 or 2001 model and showing wear, would likely belong to the cashier. The newer Ford Explorer next to it to the man in the break room. Finally, a nondescript Chevrolet sedan, an older model. That one would work.

No harm done in borrowing a ride. Calvin got up from the bench, stuffed the food wrappers into his pack, and stepped over to the Chevrolet. He reached into his pack and pulled out a cardboard cylinder. From it he unrolled two rectangular plastic sheets which fit perfectly and securely over the vehicle's front and rear license plates, now passable as Illinois plates, which would preclude tracking of the stolen vehicle by any highway or parking area cameras. Then he checked the car door and found it unlocked. Extracting a Philips screwdriver and a small needle-nosed pliers from a side pocket in his pack, he reached under the steering column and in a matter of seconds had pulled down a bundle of wires.

The young clerk inside didn't even bother to look up to see Calvin guide the Chevrolet out of the parking lot and turn onto the blacktop. South, in the opposite direction of Michigan, toward southern Ohio.

The billboard on the outskirts of Cincinnati displayed of three men in suits along with a toll-free phone number and the caption, "Life Isn't Fair. Call Us."

"Man, isn't that the truth!" Calvin rolled the window down, struggling to stay awake. Almost twenty-four straight hours without sleep. His upcoming break, in a safe and private environment, would be a relief.

Twenty minutes later, under the morning's first rays of sunlight, he pulled into a long-term parking area of the Cincinnati-Northern Kentucky International Airport. First locating the surveillance cameras which poked out from light poles, he drove around the far end of the lot and parked the purloined sedan between two larger vehicles at what would be a blind spot, removing the fake license plates and taking great care to wipe down all surfaces which he may have touched with his bare fingers. The stolen car wouldn't be found for some time; when it was, the authorities would probably assume that the thief had made his exit by catching a flight.

But flying was not on Calvin Sidney's agenda this time. Again, checking the surveillance cameras, he pulled his cap lower, stepped back, and walked away behind the row of vehicles, emerging next to a van two more rows over before approaching the shuttle bus stand, where a cluster of early morning travelers stood waiting for a lift to the terminal.

In the lower level he located a men's room and paused to regard his appearance in the mirror. A slender and finely featured young man, clean-shaven with closely trimmed dark brown hair, he could easily alter his looks to suit his various work assignments. Yesterday he had dressed professionally for his meeting in Lansing. But this morning, in jeans and a T-shirt and having been up all night, he looked rough. Disheveled. Hair mussed. He splashed water on his face and head, combed his hair, and stuffed the ball cap into his bag. He didn't want Elise to see him this way, but there was not much choice this time, due to the hurried nature of his departure from Lansing.

Yesterday's assignment for George Stanhope had gone smoothly and according to plan—until the meeting's potentially disastrous conclusion. That's when Kirsten, the Michigan legislator's associate, had grown curious about his fabricated backstory of having grown up in the Federal Hill Park locale of Baltimore. How was he to know that Kirsten had grown up near there herself?

Fortunately, by that time the meeting had been concluded and documents signed. His objectives accomplished, he had politely ended the conversation, excused himself, and exited the premises, mentally kicking himself for his carelessness in sharing too much concocted information.

He would have to watch his step for the next several days. Not that Kirsten or Representative Holtzinger would bother to check up on his identity or whereabouts, but he couldn't take any chances.

Given that possibility, he had cancelled his evening local hotel reservation. Then, from the capital complex, a twilight taxi ride to the outskirts of Lansing had brought him to a commercial area with hotels, motels, a strip mall, restaurants, and gas stations. A change of his attire in the men's room of a diner followed by a leisurely meal helped ease his lingering concerns over his situation. But with the sun having set, a ride was needed. The jovial-appearing man at the end of the counter had looked like a good option. Pete, a long-haul trucker on his way to points south in the general direction of Cincinnati, Calvin's intended destination, was happy to have some company on a long, overnight road trip.

Now, morning had arrived. Calvin had safely arrived in the Cincinnati area, with a couple of days to enjoy privately before returning to Washington, DC, for an appointed meeting with George at the end of the week.

He would be bringing George report of his mission accomplished but would also have to confess his slip-up and the potential compromise of his assumed identity. That shouldn't present any significant problem; George Stanhope was always prepared for such glitches in his operations.

This schedule fortuitously provided Calvin opportunity to visit an old friend who now lived in Cincinnati, one whom he had privately contacted several days earlier. George must never find out.

Elise understood Calvin's world. To him a kindred spirit, she had been his partner on several undercover assignments several years back, prior to and outside of the purview of any work he did for George Stanhope and the Triston Foundation.

George knew nothing of her existence, and Calvin was determined to keep it that way.

To that end he had disabled his cell phone upon leaving Lansing, using a burner phone for any essential calls. Likewise, he paid for all his purchases with currency. George had the capability of tracking the movements of his associates by pinging their cell phones and monitoring their debit and credit card transactions. If George learned of Calvin's detour to Cincinnati, needless and bothersome questions would be raised. George had no right to his personal life anyway.

Now, with time and proximity growing closer, Calvin found himself increasingly eager and, admittedly, apprehensive over this visit. Elise was bright and highly educated and had the gift of personal charisma. She could handle about any situation, taking on whatever identity, role and appearance suited the occasion. Hence her one-time role as Calvin's partner on some surreptitious assignments several years earlier.

But he hadn't seen his friend since then and knew little about her new venture in life, an earned Ph.D. and a professorship in some field related to anthropology at a university. There was catching up to do.

Calvin looked at his watch. Six o'clock. Elise would be awake by the time he got to her house. He took one more look at the mirror, picked up his bag, and walked back out of the men's room and through the terminal exit to the nearby taxi stand.

"Oh, Sid, so good to see you!" Elise threw her arms around him, calling him by the name used by his close friends and associates. "Here, come in." She stood aside, holding the door open and making a grand sweeping gesture with both arms.

Over the past hour, a circuitous string of three different taxi rides followed by a long walk had brought him to Elise's ranch-style brick house in an upscale neighborhood near the University of Cincinnati.

He stepped through the front door, alert eyes sizing up his friend's environs in a few glances. Fine hardwood flooring, crown molding, what appeared to be real oil paintings on one wall, a fine Stickley mission-style cabinet in the foyer and coffee table in the front room beyond.

Being a university professor evidently paid well enough, although Elise would have been well set financially to begin with. The financial rewards in their old mutual line of work were generous, and they both had saved and invested. For Elise, apparently enough to finance a doctoral program and maintain a fine home at the same time.

The odor of frying bacon wafted out from the kitchen.

"Yep, as promised, breakfast served," she said, watching him with a curiosity which did not escape his notice. Elise was an anthropologist. Who knew how her mind worked? Was he a subject of study?

She looked somewhat older in the face, but was still trim and well put-together, having her usual glowing expression and platinum blond hair. And her smile.

"You look shot," she said, looking him up and down by the light of the foyer.

Sid self-consciously tried to smooth his hair. "I've been up all night. Long story." He dropped his bag on the floor. "Maybe, if it's all right with you, I'll take a short nap after we eat. I'll catch you up on everything later."

"Sounds good. But now, let's eat." She led him back into the kitchen and pulled out a chair from a small round table within an alcove overlooking the back yard. "Here. I'll serve. You sit still and enjoy an intimate view of my new butterfly garden. I planted it this year, and it glistens beautifully in the first rays of sunlight. And the butterflies… oh, the butterflies! Wait until they come out a little later this morning."

His tired mind stirred. This was Elise all right. But it wasn't. A butterfly garden?

"I've never known you to be a butterfly person. What's happened to you?" He looked absently out to the garden, appraising the spread of multi-colored blossoms, shiny with morning dew, with a grudging admiration.

She laughed, that familiar delightful personality trait that so easily endeared her to others. "Oh, you're funny. You don't get me, do you. Although…" She stopped short. "How would you? It has been several years."

"Yes, it has." Sid's attention was drawn to the steaming plate of eggs, bacon, toast, and hash browns that had somehow appeared before him. But he didn't begin eating right away, feeling out of sorts. Maybe it was from lack of sleep and the stress of his flight from Lansing. But it was more than that; he had thought that he knew his old and trusted friend. Now he was not so certain.

Not knowing what to say next, he turned to his food and stuffed several forkfuls of eggs and hash browns into his mouth, gulping orange juice and coffee. Then paused for breath, setting down his fork and leaning back. "Sorry about my poor manners. I didn't realize I was so hungry."

"No apologies needed. I'm happy that I could be here for you." She continued to eye him with an intensity that made him nervous.

"George would have had my hide for such behavior. He's always been a stickler for exemplary manners, especially in public. You know how he is."

"I don't know the man, but I perceive him to be all about presentation."

All about presentation. What an interesting assessment of the esteemed founder of the Triston Foundation. What was going on with Elise?

"Okay. I give up. Who are you these days?"

"Hah, that's funny!" She laughed again.

Despite his being hungry, he forgot about what was on his plate. Was she laughing at him? "What's so funny?"

"You asked, 'Who are you these days?' The way you said that, given our former lives and line of work together, is hilarious."

"Aah, I get it." The light came on in his tired mind. "Multiple aliases and disguises and working stealth operations. But" — something about her last comment struck— "our *former lives* you say?"

"Exactly." No laughter. "What I mean is that I don't do that anymore."

"I'm beginning to get that picture. You're a university professor." Sid racked his memory. "When was the last time we worked together? Knoxville, in 2003?"

"That was it. The last time we saw each other was when I dropped you off at the bus stop… and that was over seven years ago!"

"So, what's happened to you since then?"

"Oh, it's a long story, and you're shot. Finish your breakfast. Go into the guest room and get some sleep. Then we'll talk."

A dozen or so butterflies flitted among aster, marigold, phlox, and black-eyed Susan blossoms in late morning sunlight.

"Sid, what do you see when you look at that garden?"

"Huh, nothing special. Flowers. Butterflies… Why?"

"How about a sense of wonder?"

"Wonder?" He shook his head. "I'm wondering what you're talking about."

"Please, Sid, go with me on this. Don't you ever wonder about the mystery of it all? About the flowers and the butterflies? Maybe in the way you would have marveled over something new and mysterious when you were a child?"

"Elise, you're forgetting that I didn't have a childhood. Not like most people anyway. I don't think I was ever allowed to dream or wonder about things. I was more bent on survival."

"I know. And you know that I've always sympathized with you over the hand you were dealt in life. I suffered in much the same way. But…" —she got up from her patio chair and walked over to where she could touch several blossoms— "Let's focus on the here-and-now. This backyard and the sun and warm temps. Even about your ability to see it, and feel it, and your capacity to enjoy it." Her gaze, along with her voice, seemed to drift out over the garden, as if she had been transported into another world, one which presently excluded Calvin Sidney and any history they shared.

"Elise, what's got into you? Is your new world of academia polluting your mind?"

"Nothing's 'got into me.' My perspective of our world has changed. Dramatically." She returned and sat.

"No kidding. I sensed that as soon as you started talking butterfly gardens to me this morning."

"Good. I'm glad that it shows." She jumped up again, this time going back into the house and returning with two bottles of spring water. "Here, let's drink while I elaborate."

"Elaborate? That sounds ominous."

Elise scooted her chair to an angle to where she could look more directly at him. "All I'm asking is for you to humor me for a few minutes. At least grant me the respect to hear me out. I won't bite, I promise."

"Okay…"

"Sid, my whole way of looking at our world has shifted. I'm looking through a new pair of lenses, and my eyes have been opened to the marvel of everything around us. To life's mysteries, to times and places well beyond our human capacity to grasp." She looked away again and seemed to speak to the butterflies. "Maybe even to believe in magic."

"Magic? Hold on. I am listening, but come back to earth. Give me something tangible."

"Okay." She looked down for several seconds. "How best to explain it, the fuzzy line between what we can comprehend and accept, versus that which defies our understanding, our five senses. Let me first ask you this. Do you believe in the supernatural?"

"Huh, like ESP? Or ghosts? No." Where was this conversation going? "I do believe in illusion. You know, smoke and mirrors. For me that's a normal way of doing business. But the supernatural? No way."

"Okay, understandable. But then, can you accept something as real, even if it's beyond your ability to comprehend?"

"Sure, there are a lot of things in this world that I can't comprehend, but I still believe they're real."

"Like what, for instance?" There was that penetrating look again.

Sid squirmed. "Like the notion that everything in the world is ultimately made up of atoms. You know, protons, electrons, and neutrons. I'll never see them for myself, but I do believe they exist."

"Exactly." Elise was getting excited. "You get it! And how about some other verifiable truths that are way, way out there? Way beyond even imagination?"

"Give me an example."

"All right. Here's one of my favorites. A totally random nugget of information, also scientifically verified, like the existence of atoms."

"Okay?"

"If you could strip all of the blood vessels, veins, arteries, capillaries, from your own body and stretch them out single-file, end to end, how far would they reach?"

"What have you been drinking? Or snorting?"

"Just answer the question. Take a guess. You said you would humor me."

"Okay. Hmm… maybe fifty yards. Half the length of a football field."

"Nope. The correct answer: some 60,000 miles."

"Huh, no way. You're talking like a crazy woman."

"Am I? Do you own search of medical science resources that you trust. Then tell me if I'm crazy."

"Okay, I may do that."

"Please do. Here's another one for you, even more thought provoking. I call this my 'Sex and the Lottery' speech."

"You've got my attention."

"It's like this. Each time a human sexual encounter takes place, the male contributes some 100 million sperm cells, all vying to fertilize an egg. It follows that the one sperm cell out of 100 million that wins the race is the one that produces the final human baby."

"Those are some pretty slim odds." Sid's eyes widened. "I guess you and I beat the odds. We're both in the one-in-100 million society."

"Yes, and again substantiated by medical science."

"Oh, that's right. I forgot that you've become a Ph.D. and a professor. Zapping me with all of your scholarly knowledge."

"Don't take my word for it. Check for yourself. Again, go to trusted resources. Or ask your doctor."

"Okay." Despite his contentious posture, he found himself taken aback by these figures, and by Elise's authoritative tone in conveying the information.

"I believe you will. You're bright and have a curious nature. Somehow I believe that you will verify for yourself my crazy-sounding claims."

"Yes, I'll admit that you've piqued my interest."

"And those odds don't stop with some single encounter between a man and a woman. They're compounded by the likelihood of conception over random dates and times, not to mention generational factors. You know, parents, grandparents and so on, back to the beginning of human existence. Statistically speaking, your chance of being created to sit here in my back yard this afternoon is virtually nonexistent."

"Virtually nonexistent. I guess, given the odds that we've beat, we should both be playing the lottery. That would be a shoo-in in comparison."

"Hence the title I've given my little speech," she said. "Unless"—she paused for dramatic effect— "*unless you were meant to be.* In that case, your chance of being born, of being you yourself and not someone else, would then be one-hundred percent."

So that's it! That's where this was going; it was all about religion. She was setting the hook and waiting for the right time to reel him in.

Forget any foolish notion of wonder! He wasn't going to bite. And that explained what had happened to the Elise that used to be. She had sipped of the nectar. And now she was spoon-feeding it to him. Subtly. Insidiously. Was this her reason for being so nice to him, for letting him stay with her? For making him breakfast? Just so she could preach to him? Was she still his friend?

"Hey, let's change the subject." He drained the last drops of water, set the bottle down, and pulled himself out of his chair. "I need a break."

Unwrapping the Philly cheesesteak sandwich balanced on his knees, Sid squinted into the setting sun resting on the hilltops to the west. To his front, a parade of individuals, young couples, and families passed along a boardwalk, taking advantage of the last of its rays. Beyond, the Ohio River churned along against the backdrop of the majestic Cincinnati skyline.

At his right elbow, Elise nibbled on a chicken wrap. "Thank you for not bailing out on me earlier."

"Not that I didn't consider it. You know how I get when you provoke me."

An afternoon jog through Elise's neighborhood had tempered his initial agitation following their morning discourse; he felt melancholy. Over loss. Not the pain that would accompany the breakup of a romance, but over the letting go of the notion of the close friend that he had carried in his mind for years. It had been all wrong. She had moved on, talking like some total stranger.

But they had still been friends, shared a history. He wouldn't leave. Not yet.

"Provoke?" She looked thoughtful. "I prefer to think of it as stirring. Stirring brings change. Kind of like when you stir yeast in with dough or mix chemicals or biological agents in a lab. It alters things, disrupts the status quo, makes something altogether different. For us humans, it may bring about a personal crisis of belief, a redirecting of one's path in life."

"Maybe so, but be careful what you try to stir into me. You might not like the results."

"In all fairness, Sid, what have I got to lose? You and I are on different paths, live hundreds of miles apart, and rarely see each other anymore. Whether you realize it or not, this juncture is more critical for you than you ever imagined when you called me a few days ago. Possibly my one opportunity to share my view of our world with you."

"But it all boils down to religion. That's your end game."

"Sid, I wish you would quit using that term. For purposes of our discussion, try to leave mankind's constructs of religion, its systems, its institutions, its leaders, out of it. I can't say that I embrace that term myself."

"Then, what do you call it?"

"Let's disregard the labels and definitions for the sake of this discussion. Rather, look at it like this. How can one look at the world around us and not see a divine hand at work? In that respect, that sunset is no different than the butterflies in my back yard or the many thousands of miles of blood vessels contained in your own body."

"I get that. Like the atoms." He would not give too much ground. "You're describing Intelligent Design. And I know I could find a legitimate source to back me up." He risked playfully punching her shoulder.

"Yes, it is that," she agreed. "That's a start. You brought that term up. What is *your* definition of Intelligent Design?"

"Ooh." He'd heard the term, and even bandied it about himself, but had never thought it through. "I guess I'd call it the notion that everything in the world is not random happenstance. That there is a brain behind it all, orchestrating everything."

"Oh? A brain." She dropped her mouth wide open in mock surprise. "What kind of a brain? What would it look like?"

"Man, who knows? An invisible one?"

"Aha! An invisible brain. That's the most profound thing you've said all day."

"Great! I walked right into that one."

"Then, if you can accept the possibility of an invisible brain running the whole universe, can you imagine an invisible heart doing the same thing, a heart that longs to be in relationship with you?"

"Elise!" Sid gulped the last of his sandwich and tossed the food wrapper into a nearby receptacle. "Now you're pushing me too far."

"So, what's the issue? Quit hiding from me, Sid! What's at the bottom of your resistance?"

"It's because I've patiently listened to you for the past couple of hours. You're trying to manipulate me into making something out of it all that isn't there. You're making religion out of it all. A belief system of your own choosing. And we all know that there are lots of religious beliefs in this world, each claiming to be the right one. Well, everybody can't be right. Therefore, religion doesn't work for me."

"Time out, Sid! Please quit using that term."

"Okay, sorry."

"Because, believe me, in my studies in the field of anthropology, I have learned more about the vast number of religions in the world than you could ever imagine."

"With each one of them having their own version of the truth."

"Yes, that's the rub, isn't it. But can you conceive that there is *one* absolute truth? Even among hundreds of belief systems and millions of opinions, does a singular truth, a single reality, still exist?"

"Who thinks about stuff like that?"

"Winston Churchill, for one. One quote attributed to him is this: 'Truth is incontrovertible, ignorance can deride it, panic may resent it, malice may destroy it, but there it is.'"

"Nice play on your part. But it sounds to me like Churchill didn't claim to know what it is."

"That's where you allow yourself to embrace wonderment. That's where you consider the possibility that if you do so, you will get a response. You take the first step, and then trust the real Truth to show up. Provided that you do so intentionally and sincerely."

"Okay, I hear you, but you're still talking intangibles. I'm not sure if I'm ready for this personal relationship stuff. Let's back up to where we agree. Intelligent Design. *That* I can get hold of."

"Then you do see and accept it in your mind." She reached over and tapped her fingers lightly against Sid's temple. "But you still don't have it down here." She tapped her fingers over his heart. "It's when you accept this truth with both your mind and with your heart that you will get it. That is the relationship part. And—to answer the question that has been on your mind ever since you showed up on my doorstep this morning—that is what has happened with me."

Sid let out a long breath. "Elise, I've heard everything you've said, and, while I won't tell you that I believe you or accept all that you've told me, I will admit that you are definitely not the same Elise that I remembered."

"Well, Mr. Sidney. I can tell you that neither are you the same person that you were when you arrived today. All you have to do is decide what you're going to do about it."

Matthew 5:8 (KJV)
Blessed are the pure in heart: for they shall see God.

Matthew 5:8 (AMP)
Blessed [anticipating God's presence, spiritually mature] are the pure in heart [those with integrity, moral courage, and godly character], for they will see God.

Matthew 5:8 (MSG)
You're blessed when you get your inside world—your mind and heart—put right. Then you can see God in the outside world.

THE STANHOPE FAMILY

"Bryan! Bryan!"

"What? What is it?" A muffled voice rose from beneath the covers.

Amy sat up, wide-eyed and trembling. "I've had that dream again. Flames. A man on fire! Burning up!"

"Honey, it's just a dream." Bryan sat up and held his wife, hugging her tightly until she calmed. "Try to relax."

"Maybe it was a dream. But I've never had one so vivid. What could it mean?"

ONE WEEK LATER

A full moon shone down upon five figures, shivering, but otherwise unmoving.

"It's Christmas Eve, and here I am, once again asking a lot from you and the kids. All my family together in one place. The Stanhope Clan in all its glory."

"I hear that." Bryan spoke softly, close to Amy's ear. "But remember, this year will be different. We've got an agenda. Your idea. Besides, we've made it all the way here from Illinois and nothing's happened yet."

"Not so far. But we haven't even gone into the house yet."

Amy, Bryan, and their children huddled together in the driveway. Fresh Virginia snows lay six inches deep, with temperatures in the single digits. Above, the silhouettes of stately loblolly pines against moonlit skies were unmoving in the winter stillness, while the mansion and outbuildings lay in their shadows beneath.

Snow had been cleared along the drive and to the rear of the house, and tonight a menagerie of vehicles, old and new and ranging from compact sedans and vans to four-wheel drive trucks could be seen lined up in front of the small barn in back.

Smoke curled up from the chimney and bright interior lights splashed in long rectangles out onto the snow on the front and side lawn areas, luring those outside to join in the festivities within.

"Okay, everybody." Bryan stood stiffly and pointed to the side door. "I'm cold. Let's go inside."

They trooped toward the side kitchen door in single file, Amy in the lead and Bryan bringing up the rear. She pressed the door open into the kitchen, awash with warm air and savory odors. "Hi Mom. Merry Christmas! Smells wonderful in here!"

"Oh, you're here, Amy. So nice to see all of you again. Please leave your boots in the back and hang your coats in the back closet. Everyone's in the living room." Patricia Stanhope, standing in front of the oven, wiped her hands on her apron and gave her daughter a side-hug before returning to her culinary tasks without further word, as if Amy and her family came to visit every day, not once or twice a year.

"Mom, can I help you with anything?"

"No, thank you, dear. I've got everything here under control. Maybe you and your sister can help out after dinner. For now, I just want you to go enjoy your dad and brothers. You haven't seen them since last summer."

Amy collected the children's jackets. "Kids, run along. Sounds like your cousins are in the playroom upstairs." She bent low and lowered her voice. "Take the secret stairway. Can you remember where it is?" She pointed to a doorway next to the pantry, and the three scampered off.

"These visits always make me melancholy," she whispered to Bryan. "Look at Mom, beginning to show her age. Just a reminder that the generations pass, but our old homeplace here never changes."

She and Bryan well understood the long-held tradition. The Stanhope clan had, without fail, gathered every year for Christmas Eve—beginning in the years following the Civil War—on the three hundred acres of rugged Virginia forestland which Providence had granted in the 1850s when the legendary George Jacob Stanhope first acquired the property.

"Well, face it, Honey." Bryan took off his own coat and reached for a hanger. "The house and your family traditions are deserving of some respect, given what we know about the estate's more than 140-year history."

"Imagine how scary it would have been to have Union battalions passing through the property—three different times—coming so close to home and family! With nothing touched, no harm done! There's no doubt that our home and land had been divinely protected."

"And how about Jake himself. That's another story altogether."

Patricia placed the lid on a simmering pot of potatoes and turned around. "Yes, we can be proud of Jake, making his fortune in trade and lumber businesses and all. He was a respected and shrewd businessman and community leader."

"Yes, Mother, but don't forget that he also suffered from oc-casional violent mood swings. I've been examining such behaviors. Nowadays, I believe, that would be termed manic depression."

Amy had been studying the relationship of genetic predisposition to mental health and other behavioral issues in her master's program. She'd learned that often such conditions were perpetuated by the guarding of family secrets. Who knew what secrets the Stanhope clan might be sitting on! Was there any meaning to her vivid and disturbing dream a week earlier?

"Amy, Dear. Those are just stories."

"Maybe so, but those accounts had to have endured for a reason. We all know that Jake sought various means of relief from his af-flictions, including indulgence in religious study and practice, even disappearing for a few years following the war. And to this day, no one knows where he went or what he did. And he never spoke of his time away."

"Maybe not, but he did return, and he got married and had a son through whom the family line continued. That is what matters."

"That is what *always* matters. Perpetuating the family line in all its glory."

Patricia's face darkened. "Your sarcasm has been duly noted. Listen, I've got work to do here. Why don't the two of you go out to the front room and visit."

"Sorry, Mom. I didn't mean for our conversation to go down this path. I guess that being back here in the house just stirs up a lot of emotions in me." She grabbed Bryan's elbow. "Let's go find out what's going on with the rest of my family."

Leaving the kitchen in Patricia's care, Amy and Bryan wound their way through the dining room and foyer toward the front room to behold the sight of Amy's father, William, and her three brothers, William Junior, Jeremy, and Jason, all facing each other in a semi-circle of chairs and engrossed in spirited discussion. To the side, Aunt Karen, William's sole living sibling, looked on with her characteristic amused expression.

"Be careful of what you say!" Junior pointed a warning finger. "Don't bother lecturing me on our involvement in the Middle East. You're not the President. You don't even bother to vote. What kind of an American are you?"

"Hey, lay off." Jeremy smoothed back locks of hair and adjusted his baseball cap. "You've always been the quintessential oldest child, entitled to impose your values on everyone else. Even if I had voted, you'd still be mad."

"Jeremy, in all fairness, you're never sober long enough to make a good decision. Maybe it's better that you don't vote."

"Man, you all have stressed me out. I need a smoke." Jeremy stood and fished a cigarette pack from his shirt pocket.

"Outside with that!" Junior roared, pointing back with his thumb, over his shoulder.

"I'm aware of the rules. I used to live here, too, you know." Jeremy stood, turned, and stormed into the foyer, brushing past Amy and Bryan without a word.

And a Merry Christmas to you, too, Bryan thought. He grabbed Amy's hand and led her into the front room, where they sat at one end of a sofa.

At the sound of the side door slamming behind Jeremy, Jason offered a slight nod to acknowledge Amy's and Bryan's presence, then turned back to Junior. "I see you are still driving that behemoth. Is that the way you define your masculinity?"

Junior grunted and twisted his ample form in his chair, turning to glower at his youngest brother. "Well, it's better than that wimpy-looking death trap that you drive. But, in all fairness, it probably works out just fine for getting you to the country club—oh, yeah, and to your attorney's office. How much did your divorce end up costing you?"

"Nice try, Junior. At least my wife didn't leave me for a shoe salesman," Jason sputtered.

Amy had watched the interaction among her three brothers, grieving. Their moods typically fluctuated unpredictably at family gatherings, ranging from competitive euphoria to absolute fighting and bitterness. And their physical appearances generally reflected their moods. She recalled the handed-down stories of similar behaviors among family members of past generations, wondering if such traits had carried forward to present time.

Meanwhile, Junior continued to spar with Jason. "It just comes down to common sense. In this weather I can't understand why anyone in their right mind would be out here without four-wheel drive. You're just asking for trouble."

Jason this time ignored him and turned to William, who now stood in the doorway. "Hey, Dad, since you are up, bring me another Chablis."

"You need to quit drinking so much. You'll wind up like Jeremy."

"Please, Dad. It *is* Christmas after all."

"Well… okay."

William stepped into the kitchen. "Pat, where's the Chablis?"

Patricia opened the refrigerator just as two more figures trooped through the side door into the kitchen, wrapped gifts bundled in their arms.

"Hi Mom. Hi Dad. Sorry we're late. I had to work overtime, and then we got stuck behind a wreck on the interstate." The youngest sibling, daughter Abbie, entered the kitchen, followed by her son.

She set a plastic tray on the counter. "Do you have an extra plate I can use?"

Jeremy, trailing them back into the house after his smoke break, lifted the lid from the tray. "What is this? Looks like something I'd scrape off my boots."

"It's artichoke dip, from the deli. And wheat crackers. It's the best I could do under the circumstances."

"This is Christmas, not a funeral."

"Well, guess what? I'm sorry." Abbie scowled. "You don't have to eat it."

"Oh, shush! It all looks delicious to me. Now, shoo! Give me some room to work." Patricia swept about kitchen, flinging her hands. Abbie sent her son upstairs to the playroom, and she and Jeremy followed William back out to the front room.

All the Stanhope family had arrived, the adults comfortably settled in the living room and the grandchildren upstairs. At the east end of the room was a large fireplace in which a small fire blazed. Antique brass wall sconces along three walls cast soft light everywhere. From the mantle above the fireplace hung a row of brightly colored Christmas stockings. Above them an imposing oil portrait of the family patriarch, George Jacob Stanhope, set in an elaborately carved, gold painted wooden frame. To the right of the fireplace stood a twelve-foot Christmas tree, impeccably decorated. A collection of antique nutcracker figurines adorned a long table on the left. Many of the furnishings were family heirlooms, a few dating back well into the mid-1800s.

Amy looked about the room, sadly aware that the family's numbers had diminished over the past year, she and Bryan and her parents being the only couples still together. William Junior in the midst of a divorce; Jeremy single; Jason two years divorced; Abbie in a trial separation; Aunt Karen recently widowed.

Jason looked at William. "Dad, my kid gets the first ride in the snowmobile tomorrow."

"Oh? The snowmobile? I haven't even thought about tomorrow yet."

"Hey!" Junior roared. "I think my kids should have the first ride. After all, I'm the one who bought it."

Abbie spoke up for the first time. "Sure, you did. But you gave it to Dad as a gift. It's not yours anymore. Not your decision."

"Maybe we'll draw names tomorrow," William sighed. "Truthfully, I don't know if the thing will even start. I haven't used it this year."

Patricia appeared in the doorway, ringing a small bell. "Dinner's ready! Come!"

As the line into the dining room formed, Amy studied the portrait over the fireplace. What would ol' Jake think of his descendants if he could witness tonight's gathering? His legacy.

On all previous Christmases, Bryan and Amy had patiently awaited the hour when things would wind down and they could pack up their children and leave for the serenity and privacy of a hotel room. But this year they planned to stay for the night.

Later, when the time felt right, Amy would stir the pot. She was tired of the infighting and bickering. Her family desperately needed healing, and the opportunity to talk to everybody all together generally came only once a year.

Amy and Bryan moved into the dining room, where the adults pulled up chairs and took their assigned seats around the long table, while the grandchildren were called from their play and ushered to their own table in the kitchen.

Patricia had arranged several platters and bowls of food on the table. Fine china, crystal glassware, linen tablecloth and napkins, and candlelight made for an elegant presentation. Conversation briefly subsided while dishes were passed, and plates filled. Then chatter again arose from all corners.

"My compliments to you, Mom." Jason raised his glass in a toast. "This is what I call a legitimate holiday feast! Not like Thanksgiving at Junior's place a year ago, when his wife forgot to turn on the stove, and we ended up ordering KFC for dinner! What a disaster that was!"

"Hey! At least we hosted. I don't remember you cheapskates ever doing so."

"I'd be embarrassed to have you park your contraption in front of my house. Our neighbor association would probably issue us a citation."

"Hush! It's Christmas. Abbie, pass the potatoes. Who needs more gravy?" Patricia watched over the table, half-way raised up out of her chair at one end.

"We're all fine, Mom. Please relax," Amy pleaded. "And your cranberry salad is once again a highlight. We're all fine."

"Cranberry salad," grumbled Jeremy. "Who eats that stuff anyway?"

"Maybe you'd eat it if it was spiked," Junior snipped.

Patricia straightened up, gravy boat in hand. "Christmas comes once a year, and I'm so glad and proud to have my family all together. Don't you agree, Dear?"

"Yes, Dear. Absolutely." William spoke through a mouthful of food.

Dinner continued for another hour, bickering and gloating intermingled with the clinking of glassware and dinnerware. Eventually, Amy and Abbie helped their mother and Aunt Karen whisk the serving dishes and dinner plates from the table, signaling that dessert would be served. Pecan pie and coffee followed. Then the increasing volume of chatter coming from the grandchildren in the kitchen signaled that the youngest family members were more than ready for the evening's main attraction.

At Patricia's behest, everyone adjourned to the living room for the long-awaited opening of the Christmas gifts. Like dinner, this was an orchestrated, ceremonious affair. Even the children suppressed their enthusiasm under Patricia's stern looks and took their turns opening packages, seemingly oblivious to the prevailing sarcastic and often abrasive comments of the adults.

After all gifts had been opened, Patricia ushered the children upstairs to the playroom with their new toys while Abbie moved about collecting all the scraps of wrapping paper.

Amy watched the last child disappear at the top of the main stairway, then looked nervously at Bryan. "Is this a good time?" Bryan nodded, and Amy cleared her throat loudly. No one paid any attention. Bryan then placed two fingers to his lips and let out a shrill whistle that got everyone's attention.

"Listen, please!" Amy stood and moved to an open spot next to the Christmas tree. "I know this is a little out of order for all of us, but we need to talk tonight."

Talk? The room fell into silence.

"Whatever for?" challenged Patricia, moving toward the doorway. "It's Christmas and we're all celebrating."

"Yes, Mom, I know." Amy hesitated and glanced at Bryan. "But I think that if we are all honest with each other, we'd have to say that it doesn't feel like much of a celebration. It feels more like a battle, or at least something that we must endure. That is so sad to have to say about our family, but I've been here for the past few hours and listened to virtually nonstop arguments and bickering and one-upping and the like. Why does that have to be?"

"Amy." Patricia turned to face her daughter directly. "It's okay. We just get excited and like to talk. It's just normal for us. Please calm yourself."

"But, Mom, it's *not* normal. Not for a healthy family anyway. That's my point."

"Amy, maybe you just don't feel well. You've been under a lot of pressure lately with grad school and with taking care of your family. Maybe you just need to slow down and rest."

"Mom's right. Don't be trying to sow discord, Sis!" Jason barked. "We're all fine here."

An awkward silence followed. Amy closed her eyes. Her efforts were going nowhere. Why had she bothered?

Then, finally, another voice piped up. "Wait. I agree with Sis. She's right." It was Jeremy!

Amy looked at her brother gratefully. The others looked on, but in uncertainty.

"Jeremy, why would you say that?" Patricia spoke quietly, wringing her hands in her apron.

"I'm saying that I agree with my sister. We've pretty much been fighting the whole time we've been here tonight. I'm as guilty as anyone. And this isn't the first time. It's that way whenever we all get together."

No one spoke, although several heads nodded to acknowledge his comments.

"And look at us." Jeremy spread his arms and hands to encompass the whole gathering. "Out of us five kids, only Amy and Bryan seem to have a marriage that works. What does that tell you?"

Jason snorted. "That tells me that to have a working marriage you first have to get married. It's hard to stand at the altar and recite your vows when you're drunk. That's why you're still single."

Amy, encouraged, found her voice. "Please. I'm not bringing this up to judge. All I want to know is *why?* Just why is it that we don't get along? Why do each of us seem determined to outdo each other, be critical of others' choices and lifestyles, make fun of each other? You'd think we were enemies instead of members of the same family. A pretty sad family legacy!"

Amy looked over a circle of silent, troubled faces. Faces demonstrating anger—but also shame. And fear, a shared fear. It was no secret that members of earlier generations of the Stanhopes had suffered from what were termed manic-depressive behaviors, even to the point of having to be kept closely at home or sent away for treatment. Beginning with the esteemed patriarch himself; even Jake had disappeared for a period of years following the Civil War.

Were her siblings' antics and conditions the manifestation of a genetic predisposition, a condition from which there could be no escape? If so, and if this condition was to be dealt with, they would all have to address it openly, together. Attitudes toward and understanding of mental health issues had improved in recent years; maybe there would be a way to get help.

William cleared his throat. "Family legacy, eh?"

Patricia dipped her head, avoiding eye contact with anyone.

"Okay, it's time, Pat," William began, glancing at his wife and then turning back toward his children. "Truthfully, both your mother and I do have something to say. Amy, you're right. We all need to talk, and this is a good time to start." He turned toward the fireplace, as if looking to Jacob Stanhope himself for the right words. Everyone else in the room waited in silence.

"I'll come right to the point. We all know the stories, the ones that we're not so proud of. You all know what I'm talking about, the mood swings and other behavior disorders of past generations of Stanhopes."

Murmurs of agreement.

William continued. "But you see, the conditions that you all fear cannot exist for us."

"What do you mean?" Amy asked.

"What I mean is this: not one of us here tonight is a Stanhope, not by blood anyway."

"Hold on! That's crazy! What're you talking about?" Junior's jaw dropped.

"I'm talking about genetics. There is no Stanhope blood anywhere in this room. Not me. Not your mother. Not any of you."

Patricia quietly left the room.

"But how…?" Jason's voice trailed off.

"It's a long story." William mopped his face with his handkerchief and continued. "Your mother and I have wrestled for years over when and how to explain it, and even over whether to do so at all. But we were wrong not to, and I'm afraid that we've waited too long."

"Dad, you're killing us with the suspense," Jason prodded. "Please, just get to it."

"I will, I promise. But I need to stretch, and my throat is dry. Let's take a ten-minute break, and then I'll explain everything from start to finish."

William returned to his easy chair and all the adults except Patricia took places in the front room. Silent and waiting.

"Raymond Stanhope—Uncle Ray to all of you—lived on this property his whole life, he and his older brother Herbert being the only children of Grandpa Daniel Stanhope"

Junior's jawed quivered. "Wait a minute! Did I just hear you say the *only children*? Herbert and Ray?"

"That's right. Two sons."

"Then who are you?" Jason choked.

"I'll get to that in a minute. Let's get back to Ray. Pitifully, like several of the Stanhopes he suffered from manic-depression and had to be kept out of the public for periods of time for his own good and the good of society."

"Sounds like Jake himself," Jason muttered. "The nut, so to speak, sure didn't fall far from the tree."

"Maybe so," William continued. "But Ray had been getting help and became stable enough to move back home. He and his father got along well, and he became involved in the community. That's when he met your mother" —he nodded toward the doorway through which Patricia had just made her exit— "and they soon married."

"Uncle Ray was married to Mom?" Jeremy's voice shook.

"Yes, you all heard right." William paused for emphasis, counting on his fingers. "First, I am not Grandpa Daniel's son; second, I am not Ray's and Herb's brother; third, your mother was very briefly married to Ray Stanhope."

"I'm confused." Amy clutched Bryan's hand. "Did Mom then marry you after Ray died?"

"Yes."

"Are you the father of all of us? The biological father, that is?" Abbie asked.

"Yes. Your mother and Ray didn't have any children together. I am the biological father of all five of you."

"But if you aren't a Stanhope." Junior spoke just above a whisper. "Then… who are you?"

"I was born an Ellis. William Ellis."

"And tonight you're a Stanhope. How did that happen?" Abbie's voice was strained.

"That was your Grandpa Daniel's doing," William stated, matter-of-factly.

"Our *alleged* Grandpa Daniel, apparently," Junior corrected.

"Hold on here. You're moving too fast for me." Jeremy said. "Mom was married to Ray. Let's get back to that."

"Okay, we understand that Mom and Ray were married. I assume they lived here in this house." Jason leaned forward in his chair.

"Yes, they did. And Daniel lived here with them. By that time he was a widower, old, and in poor health, and your mother and Ray looked after him. Things worked out nicely for the three of them for a time. Until one day…"

"Yes?" Jeremy urged.

"Ray received in the mail a packet, which upset him. I mean *really* upset him! He wouldn't say what was in the packet, but a couple of days later he disappeared. Just like that! Left Daniel and your mother with the house. No one knew where he went or what he did. An investigation was launched, and about a month after that his body was discovered in an apartment just outside of Baltimore. The official report concluded that his death was self-inflicted. Case closed. He was discreetly brought back and buried in the family plot in town."

"Sounds like he totally lost his mind. Was the packet ever found?" Amy asked.

"No, the packet was never seen again. Your mother knew about it. She had seen it come in the mail, but she had never seen its contents, and presumably Ray took it with him when he left."

"So, whatever was in that packet disturbed him." Jason said. "I wonder what it contained?"

"We have some theories, but that's it. Theories."

"Another family secret," Jeremy moaned. "What might those theories be?"

"We'll get to that. But, first, let's get back to me, and how I went from being an Ellis to being a Stanhope." William turned to Jeremy. "Son, since you're up, would you bring me another glass of water? My voice is beginning to give out on me again."

Jeremy left the room and returned with a glass.

William took a sip and continued. "Several months after that, your mother and I met. We fell in love with each other, and Daniel took a liking to me—treated me like a son. So, when your mother and I announced our intentions to marry, he made me a proposition. If I would agree to legally change my own surname to Stanhope, then he would leave his entire estate to me and your mother. I changed my name, and he prepared a new will."

"Whoa! Just like that?" Junior clapped his hand to his forehead.

"Yes, given that your Aunt Karen and I became orphaned in our early childhoods, my Ellis surname was not that important to me. And"—he offered a sheepish smile— "the prospect of the house and the inheritance didn't discourage me either. But please understand that I would have married your mother anyway. It was always about love, not the money."

"Wow!" Jeremy said. "Imagine someone doing such a thing. Giving away his entire estate to a man and woman who were not his true descendants, even though there *was* a blood descendant in existence."

"Hold on a minute!" Amy stuck up her hand. "What about Uncle Herb, Ray's brother? He was Daniel's elder son. Seems to me he should be living here."

"You would think so," William continued. "But Herb, we all know, was an outcast, long gone by the time that we married."

"No wonder we heard so little about him," Amy said. "He was never in the picture."

"No. Herb had gotten into trouble in his teens and left home soon after he graduated high school—and that was the last that Daniel ever saw of him. We do know that he moved to the DC area, went through several relationships, and had two sons along the way, George and Robert. But that's about it. Neither Herb nor his sons have ever had any further dealings with us."

"Didn't even care about the family's money. Can you imagine that?" Jason looked dumbfounded. "Maybe they didn't need it."

"That's possible. The Stanhopes didn't always make the best personal choices in life, but they were bright, entrepreneurial, business-minded."

"That helps explain why Grandpa Daniel did what he did," Jason continued. "He effectively disowned the three of them. Mom and Dad were the ones who cared."

"Yes. Daniel was understandably broken-hearted over their choices, but there was nothing to be done. Sadly, he died less than two years after we married."

"Daniel grafted you into the fold in order to protect the family name?" Jason asked.

"Yes, and we kept it all under wraps. It was all about the legacy and the property." William stood. "Simply that."

"So… you and Mom have been living under an assumed identity for almost fifty years! Wow!" Junior exclaimed.

"I guess you could say that."

"Then why haven't you ever told us?" Amy asked.

"I am so sorry for that," William said. "Like I said earlier, your mother and I have talked about it, but couldn't make up our minds. But, after you opened the discussion tonight, I realized that tonight was the night."

"Hmm," Amy spoke softly. "I've seen Raymond's grave in the family plot. How weird to know who he is!" She turned to her aunt. "Did you know all this? Are you really Dad's sister?"

"Yes," Karen sighed. "I knew. And, yes, I am your dad's real sister, your real aunt. I, too, was born an Ellis but changed my name when I married."

"Well, that explains why we never heard too many stories about our Stanhope grandparents," Jason said. "They weren't our grandparents after all."

"Yes," William agreed. "But the five of you are all my and your mother's children and you are all Stanhopes, even if in name alone."

Jason spoke. "It sounds like the only Stanhopes left on the face of the earth, genetically speaking, must be Herb and his sons George and Robert. Makes you wonder if he's still alive, and how his kids turned out."

"That's a scary thought," Jeremy said, finally taking a seat. "I'm not sure I want to know."

The happy laughter of the grandchildren drifted down the grand stairway from the second floor, but silence prevailed downstairs, except the clattering sound from the kitchen, indicating that Patricia was loading the dishwasher.

"Somehow, now that I've heard this, it all makes sense," Abbie said. "Oddly enough, I guess I'm not totally surprised. Maybe I had suspected it all along and didn't realize it."

"That's the thing about skeletons!" Junior said. "Somehow, they never stay put in the closet."

Aunt Karen hoisted herself out of her chair. "Wait just a minute, everyone. I, too, have something to show you… although"—she gave an ironic smile— "what you've just learned might make this easier to digest."

Seven sets of eyes, registering apprehension, followed her tired form across the room and up the stairs. After several minutes she returned, carrying a three-ring binder, and pulled her chair to the center of the room.

"Since I retired from the university, I've spent some time in the archives of the *Library of Virginia* and recently came across some information about George Jacob Stanford."

"Stan*ford*?" Amy asked. "Don't you mean Stanhope?"

"No. Stanford. Seems old Jake was born in Baltimore and moved to Virginia early in life. But then after the war, when he returned from his time away to parts unknown, his last name was Stanhope, legally changed. Sometime after that he married, and the new surname has remained ever since."

"A name change, eh?" Jeremy muttered. "Seems to be a family trait around here."

Karen chuckled and continued. "I was able to obtain photocopies of some newspaper articles from the 1860s, which I have here. Prepare yourselves!"

Nothing was said, but everyone crowded in a semicircle around and behind where she sat with the binder opened across her lap. Patricia came in from the kitchen.

"You're piqued my curiosity, Aunt Karen." Abbie leaned over her shoulder. "At least a surprise here might not be so traumatic for us. He's been dead for over 120 years."

Karen flipped through several pages, stopping at a copy of a *Richmond Dispatch* news article dated 1869.

"That looks like a long article. Just explain it to us." Jeremy squinted in attempting to read the fine print.

"I agree, Jeremy. There's a lot here," she explained. "I'll just give you the gist of it, and you can read it all for yourselves later if you so desire."

She pushed her glasses up on her nose and studied the text. "We all know that the Stanford home and property were spared from intrusion or damage by Union troops during the Civil War. What we didn't know was that the reason for such favor was that Jake had conspired with the Union Army and was secretly supplying them with provisions from his warehouses in town. He'd haul goods from town out here to his barn and then arrange to get them to the Union generals. In short, according to what I've discovered, Jake was a prosperous merchant, but he was also a traitor to the Confederacy!"

"Yikes!" Jeremy exclaimed. "And here he was, living not all that far from Richmond, the capital of the Confederacy. If that's true, he's lucky he wasn't tarred and feathered, if not executed!"

"I agree," Abbie added. "He obviously survived and managed to keep his property and money after the war. How did he manage that?"

"I don't know, and there's no explanation here. It may be that Jake had political or business connections with people who protected him. He was originally from Maryland after all, and evidently a Union sympathizer. Also, he owned everything outright. The banks had no leverage over him. However, it is interesting to note that his warehouses in town mysteriously burned to the ground soon after the war, and a culprit was never found!"

"What about slaves?" Abbie pressed. "Did he have slaves?"

"He may have. A house and property like could easily have required such labor, but there is no record of such. And this is all I have been able to find." She tapped the notebook.

Abbie spoke up. "What you've just told us about Jake makes me wonder about the mysterious packet that poor Raymond received in the mail, causing him leave so suddenly. What if its contents had revealed the truth about old Jake's real identity, his character, his actions? Just the knowledge that the family hero turned out to be a traitor could have been devastating."

"Maybe," Junior mused. "But if Ray was upset or scared enough to take his own life, there must have been something more serious at stake. I remember stories about Ray in his younger days. He was into some questionable activities and ran with a pretty rough crowd. Maybe some old secret got unearthed. Maybe he was facing arrest and prosecution."

"Or being blackmailed," Amy said.

"Or maybe one of his old enemies eliminated him and staged it to look like suicide," Jeremy added.

"Those are good theories," William concluded. "Unfortunately, it's all speculation. We'll probably never know."

As Karen snapped her notebook shut, voices arose, but this time without contention; the mood in the room had shifted.

Junior raised both arms in mock surrender. "I give up! I'm not who I thought I was. What a joke!"

"I don't know whether to laugh or cry. This is the most bizarre way to spend a Christmas that I could ever imagine." Jeremy looked up at the portrait over the fireplace. "Makes you look at old Jake in a whole different light. He's not our true ancestor. Maybe he doesn't deserve to hang over our fireplace anymore."

"You've got a point," William agreed. "I guess we could take it down and stick it up in the attic."

"I'd do more than that with it!" Junior grumbled.

Despite the late hour, conversation continued, but this time with the arguing and name-calling replaced by quiet discussion. A bottle of champaign was uncorked. Junior left the room, returning minutes later with an armload of firewood. He laid several pieces in the fireplace and nurtured the embers back to a full blaze. Then the children were invited back downstairs for a snack before bedtime. Eventually, family members arose and climbed the stairs to their respective guest rooms for the night, leaving Junior to watch the fire.

Amy pulled Bryan into the first-floor library. "What a night! When I proposed the family talk earlier, I never saw this coming."

"Hey, Amy. Don't second-guess yourself. You did the right thing."

"I suppose so. It just amazes me that all this time Mom and Dad thought they were doing us all a favor by sitting on secrets. Here they were, trying to keep peace in the family by not rocking the boat, and all they did was prolong misinformation. And we may never understand the full consequences of that."

"That's right. But tonight, you were the peacemaker, the one who introduced the potential for healing by compelling your dad to pull the covers off everything, even if it was painful."

"Thank you. I needed to hear that."

"But I'm still puzzled. If there isn't, genetically speaking, any clinical mental illness among you and your siblings, then what's the issue? Has it been the secrets themselves?"

"Possibly, in the sense that sometimes secrets aren't fully secret. Maybe somewhere along the way one or more of us kids discerned that something was amiss. Abbie earlier alluded to that possibility. Maybe Mom or Dad or Aunt Karen dropped a comment, or something else bothered us, even if we weren't consciously aware of it. Hidden sin seems to have a way of seeping out to the surface here and there, and messing with people's minds."

"Yes, that is a plausible scenario."

"And then, Bryan, there's another possible explanation, called 'self-fulfilling prophecy.' It's when people believe something so strongly that they live out their beliefs."

"Either way, it sounds like the real problem in this case was at least not genetic. That has to be great news for you."

"Yes, a huge relief!"

"So where do we go from here? What will everyone do with this new knowledge?"

"I've done my part. The rest is for everyone to figure out for themselves. But I can see that something has already changed. That was evident tonight."

Amy and Bryan ascended the stairway to their quarters.

A few minutes later, as family members upstairs drifted off to sleep in their various rooms, the grandfather clock in the foyer struck midnight. No one upstairs could hear the activity in the front room, the sounds of splintering wood and ripping canvas—followed by a sudden surge in crackling flames which brought a new and brilliant glow to the front room.

Matthew 5:9 (KJV)
Blessed are the peacemakers: for they shall be called the children of God.

Matthew 5:9 (AMP)
Blessed [spiritually calm with life-joy in God's favor] are the makers and maintainers of peace, for they will [express His character and] be called the sons of God.

Matthew 5:9 (MSG)
You're blessed when you can show people how to cooperate instead of compete or fight. That's when you discover who you really are, and your place in God's family.

FRAN

The rectangle of pale sunlight creeped upward to where it covered the top half of the exit door. That meant sunset would be in less than an hour. Everyone else would have finished supper. Mom washing the dishes; Dad tinkering with some woodworking project in the basement; Darrell and Sue doing homework.

But she, Fran Millwright, would spend the evening by herself, seated on a simple wooden chair with nothing to do or to look at. A prisoner in her own home.

A single ceiling fixture shed dim light over her space, empty except for the chair on which she sat. To the left of the room's only entrance, a second, narrow doorway had been cut into the wall to allow direct access to a half-bathroom.

Beyond the entry door at least one guard would be within earshot, probably Mother at this time of day. That door was not locked, but there was no point in opening it, short of the house being on fire. Doing so would increase her sentence, her confinement in what used to be the house's three-season porch, until most of the windows were walled over a few years ago to help keep out the cold Minnesota winters. Now the twelve-by-twelve space, its two remaining windows, narrow, horizontal, and high along one wall, served as Marshall and Pauline Millwright's *Solution*.

With evening approaching, Fran knew that her father's knock was imminent. He was the final household authority on matters of discipline. She would be allowed out, with just enough time for a brief review of her transgressions, then to finish her own homework before getting ready for bed. It had been a long day, probably more than five hours spent in solitary confinement from the time she had returned from school. No supper tonight; a plastic cup on the bathroom sink for drinking water; she would be allowed to eat tomorrow at breakfast.

Then the anticipated tap at the door, which opened a crack.

"Fran, are you ready?"

"Yes, Dad." She rose and followed him out into the front room. Mom lay nestled in her chair in the living room, her nose in a magazine. Darrell and Sue were not in sight, probably in their own rooms.

"I'll be heading up for the night." She kept her eyes lowered, hoping to avoid any further reprimands from either of her parents; such lectures were pointless anyway; they would not change what she had observed and believed, what she knew to be true.

Mother's head popped up from her magazine. "What have you learned tonight, Fran?"

"I've learned to be careful how I speak."

Mother nodded. "Yes. You do realize that the kinds of questions you raised at school today could be considered accusatory, maybe even slanderous. The principal warned your father as much. You could put yourself, or us as your parents, in trouble. Fortunately for you, we live among gracious and forgiving people."

"Yes, ma'am."

"Your father and I didn't raise you children to be that way. Just because you're getting older and entertaining certain notions in your head doesn't give you the right to be nosing into other people's business. We simply won't put up with that. There will be consequences, both here at home and out in the community."

"Yes, ma'am."

Fran climbed the stairs to her own room. The next thirty minutes or so would be devoted to algebra. Then bed, and an attempt to sleep. Sleep would not come easy… but she would wake up to a new day, and the chance to again see both Tony, and, later, Leann. The only people in Thistle Junction, besides herself, that understood.

"Hey Fran." At his locker between morning classes, Tony called and waved. "How did it go for you at home last night?"

"The whole evening spent under household arrest. The price I pay for asking what was apparently the wrong question. Thanks for giving me the rest of your lunch yesterday. I think that's what got me through."

While having been in school together from first grade, the pair had become close friends over only the past two years. As Tony's lab partner in their junior year biology class, Fran had spent hours tutoring him so that he could ace that class, ensuring his parents' permission for him to continue playing basketball and running track. This spring, with graduation for Thistle Junction's High School class of 1977 just weeks away, both Fran and Tony were counting down the days.

During that time the two, while not romantically inclined toward each other, had discovered their shared observant and inquisitive natures, questioning and occasionally challenging anything that didn't make sense in their small world, including several of the rules and guidelines laid down by teachers or other school officials.

"Fran, I hate that for you. Do you know who squealed?"

"I'm convinced it was Mr. Barnes. He probably told the principal, who then called my dad."

Tony laughed. "You've never been short on curiosity. Asking Barnes if he had enjoyed his weekend sure got a reaction. And I can promise you that the class loved it, even if none of them say anything. People pay attention. I hear their comments."

"Well, it was an innocent enough question and shouldn't have made Mr. Barnes nervous or angry, except that we both know where he really was. So, we learned that he is capable of lying."

"Yes, he is," Tony agreed. "And I know, as an eyewitness. I couldn't believe it when I came across him and Bonnie Lantz down behind Parker's Mill Saturday morning. Lucky for me I spotted them before they could see me. But that also meant that I couldn't even get to my favorite fishing hole."

"If you remember, I've told you that I overheard something that he said last fall. I didn't understand what he was talking about, but I gathered enough to know that the guy keeps secrets."

"Well, you don't seem to worry about having a target on your back."

"Tony, you know me. That's just part of my DNA. The more that my folks or anyone else around here try to tell me that I don't know what I'm talking about—well, that encourages me. I didn't question Mr. Barnes to create trouble. I just wanted to see how he would answer."

"That's fine, but what if ol' Barnes figures out that you're on to him? He may do whatever it takes to save face."

"Yes, that could make things interesting.

"Hi, Fran. The usual?" Leann Schoenheider turned from where she had been arranging soup cans along a shelf. Fran's close friend, the sole owner and operator of the Thistle Junction Pantry, was a fixture in the small community, and was, except for Tony, the one person in town in whom she could confide.

Unlike most of the residents of the Junction, including several generations of Fran's own family, Leann was an outsider, having inherited the small grocery from an uncle after his sudden death. A few years earlier, she had come to town from St. Paul, intending to stay long enough to sell the business and settle his affairs. Instead, she found that she enjoyed the routine of running the store in the small community. She stayed, becoming attached to her new, small world despite its peculiarities.

"Sure." Fran walked over to a cooler, pulled out an orange soda, and snapped it open. "What's new in town?"

"Not much. Not that anyone's shared with me anyway. Are you shopping for your mom today?"

"She's experimenting with another casserole recipe for dinner, which works out for me just fine, because it gives me reason to stop in. Your store is about the only place in town outside of school that she lets me go without supervision. Probably because you're right on my way home, and because you keep complimenting her on her flower garden. She likes you."

Leann laughed. "How about that. Hey, don't you turn eighteen next week? That should make things a little easier for you."

"Yes. Oh, it will. I haven't figured out all the details yet, but I will continue to do my part to be a good citizen to our little community."

"Well, my friend, whatever you decide to do, you know that I believe in you."

"Thanks, Leann."

The Millwrights had long been among Leann's regular customers. But in recent months Fran and Leann had begun confiding in each other during Fran's frequent after-school stops; Leann treated Fran in a way unlike her own parents or others in town ever would: as an adult. A mature-minded, thinking adult, set apart from the general population of their small community.

"Fran." Leann looked around to be sure the store was otherwise unoccupied. "I know how you think."

"Everyone in town knows how I think. That's why some folks don't like me and others are afraid of me. Even so, a small number still seem to trust and appreciate me."

"And I count myself among that last group; I respect and trust you a lot. For that reason, I need to tell you about something that's happened."

"Yes, what is that?" Intrigued, Fran set the groceries on the counter and glanced toward the entryway. No one in sight.

"Fran, there's something illegal going on around here, and it's got me scared to death."

"Oh? That doesn't surprise me any, but what is it?"

"The truffles."

"The truffles? The Thistle Junction Truffles? You're joking."

"I'm serious."

"How did you come up with that?"

Despite their being alone in the store, Leann again looked around before answering. "It was something that happened last week. You know I sell the candy here."

"Yep, it's a local favorite, the pride of Thistle Junction. My dad used to work at the plant." Fran pointed over to a display case along one wall which held rows of red and cream-colored candy boxes, each sealed in shrink-wrapped plastic. "So, what happened?"

"Their delivery guy came by on Monday morning, just like he always does. Parked his truck out front and brought in a couple of cartons of the candy boxes to restock."

"Okay?"

"But as he was pulling boxes from one of the cartons and placing them on the shelf, he happened to drop one."

"Ooh, did it break open?"

"No, it didn't. But it landed upside-down, and when he leaned down to pick it up, he saw something on the bottom. And what he saw made him upset."

"What did he do?"

"Well, he couldn't do much; I was right there watching. But I could tell that he was nervous. Then, he began pulling the newly delivered boxes back off the shelf and putting them back into the carton, in a big hurry."

"And… let me guess. You, in your famously polite and innocent manner, asked him what was going on."

"You bet I did." Leann chuckled. She bent down and brought out a truffle box from under the counter. "He looked just like the kid that got caught with his hand in the cookie jar. So, while he had his back turned for a second, I switched out this box which he had just delivered with one that had already been on the shelf."

"You secretly traded one from your display for one of the new ones he had brought in?"

"Yes. And then he said something like, 'Sorry, Leann. I've gotten your order mixed up with another.' He repacked the carton, hauled it back outside and came back in with another, which he then unloaded."

"Sounds like he pulled the wrong carton off the truck the first time."

"That makes sense. Except that his looking at the bottom of one of the individual boxes would not have clued him in on that. It should have been the labeling on the cartons themselves."

"True. And since all the boxes of truffles are the same, he could easily have substituted one of yours at the next delivery stop. No need to repack a carton."

"Exactly. Which then led me to wonder if all of the boxes were *not* the same." Leann turned the box over so that Fran could see the bottom. "So, I looked for myself. See this?" She pointed to a red stamp of the letter *D*, the only printing evident on the otherwise plain white surface.

Fran nodded. "Okay, a stamp. So what?"

"This is where things get scary." She lifted the lid of the box. Inside were four rows of truffles, all neatly lined up in a plastic tray insert. Leann lifted the tray out of the bottom of the box, revealing a small packet filled with white powder and taped to the inside bottom of the box.

"Ooh!" Fran whistled. "Drugs? Is that what cocaine looks like?"

"I don't know, but it's possible." Leann walked over to the shelf and retrieved another box so that Fran could see its bottom. "See, this one has the letter *L*."

"So, apparently you're supposed to have only L-stamped boxes in your store."

"I checked, and all of the boxes on my shelf are stamped with an L. And guess what? No packets of powder inside. I opened three or four of them to make sure."

"That, Fran, explains the actions of the delivery man." Leann put the L-stamped box back on the display case and stashed the D-stamped one back under the counter. "I can read faces. Whether he was aware of the contents or not, the guy at least knew I was not supposed to have this box." She pointed down behind the counter.

"Aah, smuggling drugs in the candy boxes." Fran's thoughts were racing.

Leann looked at her. "I know how you think. You're wondering about what's going on out at the Thistle Junction Truffle plant."

"Exactly!" Fran's eyes suddenly widened. "Oh my! That may explain it."

"Explain what?"

"My dad. My dad used to work there in sales, until he was let go a couple of years ago."

"Your dad? Marshall Millwright let go? He's a faithful and hard worker. That doesn't make sense."

"No, it doesn't, and he would never talk about why. Said it was a financial decision by the owner. But I'm beginning to wonder…"

"Maybe your dad discovered something, or wasn't willing to go along with some plan or idea."

"Maybe. Like I said, he would never talk to any of us about it, even my mom. We assumed it was because the plant was in financial straits for a while, almost bankrupt. But I'm thinking there might be more to it. Maybe my dad was even threatened to keep his mouth shut."

"That's a frightening possibility. Admittedly, I've long had concerns about the plant's operations." Leann scowled. "Hank Avery is the production manager, and we all know Hank. The guy doesn't fire on all pistons, even when he's sober, which isn't too often. He wouldn't necessarily know if someone was adding packets of illegal drugs to some of the candy boxes."

"Or he may be aware." Fran recalled something Tony had said. Her friend was the second shift custodian at the plant on the weekends and had complained to her about the lax quality control measures. "I know that the production process and products are subject to routine inspections and testing. Ol' Hank may be willing to pull a coverup or look the other way if someone threatened him."

"Or paid him off." Leann shook her head. "Don't forget that Hank's a cousin to both the mayor and to the sheriff. You and I do have our suspicions about those two."

"Not to mention my civics teacher, Mr. Barnes. And there may be others."

"Right. They're not going to bother Hank."

"How long do you think this has been going on?"

"I have no idea." Leann's expression turned sorrowful. "Although I'm glad to know that apparently I've been selling only L-stamped boxes, those without the drugs."

"While the D-stamped boxes are probably shipped out to select customers."

"I believe you're right. It's a good way to distribute the goods and make some serious, tax-free income. Enough to pull the plant out of potential bankruptcy."

"Wow, if that's the case, we're sitting on some pretty serious evidence," Fran exclaimed. "We've got to notify someone that we can trust."

"Yes. Unfortunately, where I've torn off the plastic seal and opened this box, it is no longer evidence. The authorities would claim that I added the packet myself. And, we don't even know what the stuff is."

The ringing of the bell over the door halted the discussion. "Oh, hi Sheriff!" Leann chirped, smiling at the man in the entryway. She looked back at Fran and rolled her eyes. "Speak of the devil," she whispered.

"Good afternoon, Leann. Hi, Fran." Sheriff Irvin Avery picked up a jug of milk before approaching the checkout counter. "Fran, good to see you today. I guess school must have just gotten out. Are you shopping or just visiting?"

"Shopping, Sheriff. Just picking up a few things for Mom."

"All right. Tell your folks hi for me."

"Will do." Fran paid Leann for her groceries and left the store. She didn't need the sheriff informing her folks that she had any relationship with the owner of the Pantry beyond being just a regular customer.

"Hey, you look a year older! How did your grand celebration go this weekend?" Tony playfully punched Fran's shoulder while they stood in line going into the lunchroom.

"It's over. I prefer to call it my liberation day, not my birthday."

"My congratulations to you. Now you've got more rights. Legal rights."

"I do." Fran lowered her voice. "At least my folks have agreed not to employ their juvenile means of punishment any longer. They both seem to have accepted the reality of my adulthood."

"Aah, yes. Their infamous Solution Room. But how's that going to work out? You still live in their house."

"True. But you know I don't plan to stay here after graduation. I'm going on to college next fall and may even spend this summer away."

"Making your grand escape. I'm happy for you. But your poor mom won't go for that. She's determined that you would marry some guy from around here and stay put. She wants grandchildren."

"So she tells me."

"Oh, hey, Fran." Tony suddenly became cautious. "I've got to talk with you. Privately. When can we meet?"

"Right after school, in the home ec room. It should be empty."

"Sure. Track practice starts at four, but we should have a few minutes."

"Good. See you then."

At three-twenty the final bell rang, and students made their ways to their lockers, to either leave for the day or go on to after-school activities. Fran and Tony slipped into the unoccupied classroom and closed the door.

"Fran, I heard something last night that you will find very interesting. The stuff that movies are made of."

"I'm listening."

"It was last night at the plant."

Fran's heart skipped. *The truffle plant!* "What was it? Tell me." Should she say anything about what Leann had learned about the candy boxes? She decided to wait, for both Leann's and Tony's sakes.

"Last night I took my usual break about nine o'clock. Normally I go into the break room to eat my snack. But I'd forgotten it in the truck, so I walked out to the parking area behind the plant. And then just stayed out there; sat in the truck in the dark, eating my sandwich. Enjoying peace and quiet... until the truck pulled up."

"A truck?"

"Terry McCall, the company owner, pulled up and parked a few feet away from where I was sitting, but without seeing me. I thought it odd for him to be there that time of night. Then Jacob Welles drove up and parked next to him, driver side to driver side."

"Jacob Welles? The mayor?"

"Yep. They both rolled down their windows and talked freely, oblivious to my being close enough to hear everything. And, boy, did I learn something! Fran, did you know that Mayor Welles had put a ton of his own money into the operation, to help save the plant from bankruptcy?"

"No! I had no idea. That, in effect, could make the mayor a joint owner. He and Terry are second or third cousins you know."

"Why should that surprise me? But the two of them carried on for some time about a new supplier from down south somewhere. Then Terry agreed to make a road trip in a few days to pick up more product. Somehow, it didn't sound like he was talking about candy ingredients."

Fran's head was spinning. It was all beginning to make sense! Then she recalled Leann's comment about needing a sealed box of candy for evidence to present to some authorities. Tony might be her best means of getting her hands on that.

"Hmm. Do you think they're running a drug operation?"

"Could be a possibility. Unfortunately, I didn't hear anything conclusive, but the fact that the two of them were meeting late at night out in the parking lot looks pretty suspicious."

"I agree! It's a good thing they didn't spot you. You could seriously be in danger."

"I've thought about that more than once."

Fran then decided to enlist her friend's help. "Tony, since you've demonstrated your ability to work in the shadows, I have a big favor to ask of you."

"That sounds ominous."

"Given what you've just told me, I am wondering if you could somehow get your hands on a couple boxes of candy, without anyone knowing about it."

"I guess I could, fairly easily. Why?"

"Sorry, I'm not yet at liberty to say. But I promise to explain later."

"No problem. I trust you."

"Thanks. And there's just one more thing."

"Yes?"

"Make sure that you get at least two boxes. They have to be sealed and have the letter D stamped on the bottoms."

"The letter D? I don't understand."

"That's because there are two kinds of boxes, some with D-stamps and the others with L-stamps. I must have the D-stamped ones."

Tony looked puzzled but didn't ask any further questions. "Okay. I'll see what I can do."

During her walk home from school, Fran thought about Jacob Welles, given the new information that Tony had just shared. Thistle Junction's mayor lived on a twenty-acre hobby horse farm on the edge of town and had recently purchased a condominium in Florida. How could he afford such a lifestyle on his salary at the grain elevator?

More questions nagged. Where did Mayor Welles come up with the kind of money needed to save the truffle plant from bankruptcy? Had he somehow tapped into City funds? Or, from the elevator? Was he supplementing his income in some illicit activity through the truffle plant?

Furthermore, Mayor Welles was a cousin to not only Terry McCall, but to Hank Avery, the plant manager, and Sheriff Avery. Perhaps others.

She would do some more investigating.

Tony, leaning on his mop, looked up and down the hallway at the back of the truffle plant. Three doors, those leading into offices, were shut and locked. Another door to the break room stood open, light spilling out into the hallway; next to it a rest room; double doors at the end of the hall opened into the main production area where the truffles were made and packaged.

At this hour the other employees on site were plant manager Hank and five others working in production, all involved in hand-packing individual truffles into their boxes and sending them through the shrink-wrapping machine. Hank would be in the break room, sipping from the flask he kept in his locker and looking at some hunting or fishing magazine.

This was his opportunity to locate boxes of candy, so that he could pick them up later.

Cartons of finished product were stored in a climate-controlled room at the back of the building, from where they were loaded onto delivery trucks during the day shift. Using his master key, Tony stepped into that room, pulling his mop bucket behind him. Most of the candy was packed in cartons stacked on shelves, but several individual boxes rested on a table close to the door. Tony lifted one of these and looked at the bottom.

"L," he breathed. This wouldn't work. Fran had said she needed two of the D-stamped ones. He flipped over each of the others. All L-stamped. He examined the cartons on the shelves, which similarly displayed L-stamps.

There had to be some D-stamped boxes somewhere. If not here, then in either Terry's or Hank's office.

Tony mopped the floor of the storage room before moving back into the hallway, working his way down the corridor with the mop and bucket. Hank appeared in the break room doorway, an unlit cigarette in his hand and the strong odor of whiskey on his breath.

"I'm going outside," he said, lumbering past Tony and pushing open the back exit. Hank's smoke break would take at least five minutes, and probably closer to ten. This was the chance to get into his office. Planting the mop and bucket right beside Hank's office door, Tony used his same master key to unlock it. Once again surveying the hall, he stepped in and turned on the light.

The space was small and sparsely furnished, a metal desk and two chairs against the right-hand wall. To the left a large metal cabinet. Fortunately, no windows. Tony twisted and pulled the handle to the cabinet door and it swung open. On a lower shelf were two stacks of candy boxes, probably thirty boxes altogether. Tony lifted one and turned it over.

A D-stamp!

Tony grabbed the top box from each of the two stacks, making sure they both had D-stamps. Hank would not notice two missing boxes, especially in tonight's inebriated state. He shut the cabinet door, turned out the light, and exited the office, pulling the door shut and locked behind him.

At the same time the back exit door opened, and Hank stepped back in. "Forgot my lighter," he mumbled. "And my truck keys."

Too close! Heart pounding, Tony set the two candy boxes on the floor behind the bucket and made a show of wringing out his mop while Hank filed past him and went into his office, reappearing seconds later with his keys and a lighter in hand. Then he strode back outside.

Breathing more easily and again surveying his surroundings, Tony carried both candy boxes into the break room and secured them in his own locker. He would sneak them out to his own truck once his shift was over.

"Hey, Bonnie."

"Hi, Fran. What brings you downtown? Do your folks know you're here?"

"No, but they don't mind. Since my eighteenth birthday, they've lowered some of their restrictions on my activities."

"Well, you're certainly embracing adulthood." Bonnie Lantz, the city administrative assistant, nodded, not looking entirely pleased with her young visitor.

"Bonnie, I came to ask you a question. Kind of a business or government question."

"How can I help?"

"I'm taking a civics class in high school, Mr. Barnes's class."

Predictably, the woman winced slightly at that name.

"We're learning about government accountability and audits and all that sort of thing. And I'm just wondering if Thistle Junction ever has its finances and operations inspected or audited by an outside, independent source."

Bonnie fumbled with a paperweight on her desk while looking around the room. "That's a very interesting question, coming from a high school student. Perhaps you need to talk with Mr. Welles. But he's not available today."

"Hmm. No, I don't necessarily need to take up the mayor's valuable time. But I need a real-world perspective on what we're learning in school. You happen to be the best resource available to me."

"Well…" Bonnie set the paperweight down. "That would be the folks up in St. Paul. The Office of the State Auditor."

"Okay, how often do they do an audit?"

"Out here on site, once annually. But we also file reports at other times of the year."

"Do they audit Mayor Welles personally?"

"Why Fran! That kind of information is none of your business!" Bonnie's eyes narrowed and she began tugging on an earring.

"Sorry. I understand. It's just that we're studying local government in my civics class" —she couldn't resist— "you know, Mr. Barnes's class. I do take that class very seriously."

Bonnie looked away, avoiding Fran's stare.

The poor woman is probably wondering if I know about her little secret.

"Well, to answer your question," she finally replied. "I don't know who does the mayor's taxes. And, even if I knew, I don't know that I would tell you. But I'm going to tell Mr. Welles that you asked. Maybe he'd like to answer your questions himself."

"That's fine." Fran enjoyed watching the woman squirm. "Thank you for your time, Bonnie. You've been more helpful than you realize."

"You're welcome, Fran. I'll be sure to pass along your questions to Mr. Welles."

"Please do." Fran skipped out the door.

Flashing blue lights appeared in the rear-view mirror. Atop a familiar vehicle.

"Great!" Fran looked at her speedometer. Had she been speeding? She resignedly pulled to the side of the road. Only the second time ever that she had been allowed to drive her mother's car on her own, on this occasion to visit her aunt across town.

Through her mirror she watched Sheriff Irvin Avery heave himself out of his squad car and amble up to the driver side window. The sheriff would not be offering any mercy. He'd probably heard about her visit yesterday to the city offices.

"Hi, Sheriff." She lowered her window, blinking in bright sunlight at the officer who towered over her.

Avery, scowling, scribbled on a pad. "Fran, did you know you were over the speed limit? And, that you didn't come to a full and complete stop at that last stop sign?"

"Sorry."

"Here you are, an adult. Real proud of yourself and acting like some hot-shot, and then wind up getting ticketed on your first venture out on your own. How long you been driving anyway? Less than a year?"

"Something like that. Sorry." Inwardly, she seethed. The sheriff never tickets his cousin Hank, even when Hank drives drunk through town. But she held her tongue.

He tore off a slip and handed it to her. "Thirty-five dollars this time. Be careful what you do. Don't let me catch you again." He turned and ambled back to his car.

She started the car and continued toward Aunt Jean's house, this time well below the speed limit. Complete, dead stops at stop signs. Turn signals at every turn and lane change. Like everything else in her current world, alertness and circumspection in her driving practices would be essential.

The sheriff's traffic stop was pure retaliation. That was obvious. She would have to watch her step. Her folks would know about her infraction even before she returned home, which would likely mean an end to her borrowing the family's cars for the time being.

But she could not deny her desire to seek out and expose any illegal activity or other injustice. The traffic stop proved that yesterday's visit to City Hall had struck a nerve. There would be no quitting until any criminal dealings by Thistle Junction's leadership were brought to light.

Time was running out. Graduation was weeks away, after which she would seek a new life elsewhere. But Fran would not leave until she had taken steps to ensure that her parents and her siblings could continue to live here in safety.

"Yes, Fran. Do you have a comment?"

"Another question, Mr. Barnes. About accountability of local government." Fran suspected that Bonnie had notified him of her recent visit to the city offices. But she needed to know how her civics teacher would respond to the same line of questioning.

The classroom grew quiet; her classmates had come to enjoy the dynamics whenever she raised issues which unnerved their civics teacher. This time Mr. Barnes did not disappoint; he stiffened perceptibly, the muscles in his face and neck tightening. "Okay, Fran. Ask away. We're all listening."

"Who holds local governments accountable for the way they conduct business? You know, how they manage money, implement local ordinances, enforce the law, and so forth. Are they held to standards by some higher authority?"

"Well, Fran, that's a very interesting and provocative question. Why do you ask?"

"Because this is civics class. It's what we study in here."

Soft laughter flowed about the room.

"Okay…" Barnes turned and stepped behind his desk. "Well, I would say that state government has authority over our communities in that regard."

"Then, how does the state know what's going on locally, say, right here in Thistle Junction?"

"The city routinely submits tax returns and other reports. And the state sends people out to perform audits."

"Then, they would know if, say, some city official was negligent or incompetent in his or her duties? Or embezzling funds?"

More suppressed laughter.

"You're correct." Barnes cast an irritated look around the room. "That's what an audit is for. To give assurance that financial figures are correct, and that business and accounting practices are done properly."

"How about the fraud situation over in Cedarfield a few years ago? Was that criminal activity revealed by an audit?"

"Oh, I don't remember exactly how that all went down. It may have been from an audit. Or it may have been some meddling citizen blowing the whistle. That was several years ago."

"One more question, Mr. Barnes. If some citizen became aware of unethical or illegal activity in her community, how could she report such suspicions? Or, to what higher authority would she appeal?"

The bell rang.

"We're out of time today." Barnes looked relieved. "See you tomorrow."

"Well, the poor guy was saved by the bell this time, wasn't he?" Tony chuckled quietly at Fran out in the hall. "But you unnerved him this time. You know that there could be repercussions, more than just getting a traffic ticket."

"I know.'" Fran shrugged. "I hate that it has to be this way, and I know that it may cost me. But I've never forgotten what I overheard Mr. Barnes say last fall. On the phone after school one day, not realizing that I could hear him. He was threatening someone. Tony, what if Mr. Barnes had become aware of some illegal activity by the mayor or the sheriff or Hank? What if he was blackmailing them?"

"Wow! This just keeps getting more tangled."

"I'm not going to quit until I've uncovered whatever secrets this town holds. And, by the way, thank you for picking up those candy boxes. Don't worry. Your name will never come up as my accomplice. I promise."

"Thank you!" He bowed slightly. "Just glad I could help. You are indeed a woman on a mission."

"I have to be, Tony. There are innocent people living here, my parents and younger brother and sister in particular. You know that my dad used to work at the plant, and then was let go for unexplained reasons. What if he knows something and has been threatened to keep his mouth shut? That puts my whole family at risk. Unlike you and me, they don't get to leave in a few weeks."

"Fran, what are we going to do with you?"

Marshall, Pauline, and Fran sat around the dining room table. The two younger siblings had earlier been ordered to their rooms until the "discussion" with their older sister had been accomplished.

"Mr. Barnes is unhappy because I ask some fair questions in his class. Isn't that what school is for? To encourage questions?"

"Yes, it is, Fran," Marshall replied. "But the way you framed your questions today evidently sounded accusatory. According to Mr.

Barnes, you were implying that our local authorities were engaged in criminal activity."

"An innocent person would have had no issue with the questions I asked. The fact that Mr. Barnes was bothered enough to complain to you about me should tell you something."

"How can you say such a thing?" Pauline's eyes narrowed.

"Because personal accountability, transparency in the ways we conduct our work and our lives, is important for all of us, especially for those in authority. Don't you agree?"

"That sounds reasonable. So, who doesn't meet your standard? Give us a concrete example, not just hearsay or your opinion."

"Here's one. Hank, who holds a management position up at the candy factory. Everyone knows that he's an alcoholic, even drinks on the job. No one holds him accountable. Dad, have you ever wondered how he has managed to keep his job while you were let go?"

Marshall winced. "Yeah…well, poor Hank has had a rough go of things. They're lucky to have him; he's been a faithful employee for more than fifteen years. And he's a deacon at church."

"And he's the mayor's cousin. So, he gets a pass? Even when he drives through town impaired?"

"Fran! Watch your tongue!"

"Here's another puzzle. How does Mayor Welles maintain his lifestyle? Tell me that. A twenty-acre hobby farm? A condo in Florida? A home furnished from the Twin Cities' finest stores? I doubt that his day job at the grain elevator pays all of those kinds of bills."

Pauline's whole body shook. "Fran, how can you make statements like that, about things that you have no way of knowing? Things that are none of your business?"

"That's because I pay attention, Mom. I have eyes and ears, and I use them. I listen to what other kids say. And to what adults say."

"Fran." A look of fear flitted across Marshall's face. "You're a bright young lady, but at times you can be too inquisitive for your own good. As your father, I'm respectfully asking you to hold your tongue around here. What you're doing is upsetting others in town. That could get you in trouble. Big trouble."

"Thanks for the warning." Fran stood. "All I'm doing is seeking after what is right and what is true. I'm observant and persistent, and—I'll admit—at times too blunt for some people's tastes. Always have been. Your little room in the back of the house is evidence of that. But I'm going to find out the truth about a lot of things around here, and I won't be bullied. Not by Mr. Barnes or the sheriff or anyone else."

"Hi, Leann!" Fran strolled into the pantry.

"Oh, Fran. It's you. Are you shopping for your mom tonight?"

"No. Just stopped by to chat before heading home."

"In that case, I'm so glad you stopped." Leann was not her usual cheery self, even appearing frightened. "Please come back here. Now!" She motioned with her hand, her head swiveling about to be sure they were alone.

"What is it?" Fran became nervous.

"Let's go back to my office." They both stepped through a doorway in the back of the store, Leann leaving the door open just a crack. "You're in trouble, Fran."

"And… what else is new?"

"No, I mean real trouble this time. Hank Avery was in here a while ago. Drunk and running his mouth, which he frequently does when he stops in. But this time he was talking about you."

"Me? Why?"

"Well, let's think about this. You've stirred up your civics class—*Mr. Barnes's* civics class, no less. And you paid a visit to the mayor's administrative assistant. The word spreads around here. You've made some people very nervous and upset. They're out to get you. To discredit you. Destroy your reputation."

"How?"

"They're going to set you up, and they've hatched a plan. Hank, the dimwit that he is, told me all about it."

"I can't wait to hear it."

"They're going to accuse you of shoplifting from the drug store. Haul you in for questioning and plant some prescription bottles on you."

"Ooh! That *is* serious." Fran suddenly felt faint. She could be processed and tried as an adult. "It wouldn't surprise me if even Mr. Phelps, the pharmacist, is also involved. When or where is this supposed to happen?"

"Probably either at school or at your house, the two places they know they can find you. I don't know when, but it could be as soon as this evening."

Fran plopped down in a chair. "Okay. Let me think about this."

The front bell jangled. Leann peered out. "I've got a customer. Stay put and don't make a sound." She turned out the ceiling light and stepped out, closing the door. Fran sat in the dark, listening to the muffled sounds of polite conversation. Within five minutes Leann returned, a can of orange soda in hand.

"Look, Fran." She handed her the soft drink. "I've got an idea to get both you and our boxes of candy out of here. To trusted friends that can help."

"Okay." Fran gratefully sipped her drink, holding the can with trembling hands. "After what you've just told me, I'm open to about anything."

"You stay right here. I'll bring you a sandwich. I close up at nine o'clock tonight. Then I'm getting you out of here. After dark. No one will know."

The bell out front rang again. Leann switched off the office light and stepped out. Fran sat still in the dark, listening. The customer's voice was familiar. Not friendly.

"Leann." It was Sheriff Irvin. "How are you? How's business?"

"Fine, Sheriff. How about yourself?"

"Okay. Keeping busy. By the way, have you seen Fran Millwright today? I know she stops in here from time to time."

"Oh, Fran? She does shop here, regularly. If I see her, can I give her a message?"

"Yes, please ask her to get in touch, either with me or with her parents. Something's come up at the Millwright home, something with her brother, and they're trying to locate her."

"Ooh, that sounds like trouble. Is it serious?"

"No. Thank you for your concern. It's an urgent personal matter, and Fran's involvement is needed. I can't say any more about it."

"I understand. I will pass your message on to Fran if she comes by."

"Thank you, Leann."

The clinking of the bell indicated that the sheriff had left. A minute later Leann returned, a wrapped sandwich in hand. "I guess you heard all that. That's our trusted sheriff for you, lying through his teeth. Even more reason to get you out of here."

The hours in Leann's small office passed slowly. Fran sat still, hardly daring to breath in the dark while Leann waited on customers, making pleasant conversation while ringing up their orders during the early evening's surge in business. Then stopping back to visit whenever she could. The woman was smooth! No one would ever suspect that she was harboring a fugitive from the local authorities!

Even Sheriff Irvin stopped back one more time, asking about Fran.

"Sheriff, I told you I would speak to her if I saw her. I take it you haven't located her yet?"

"No, Leann. And her folks are getting worried. It's not like Fran to up and disappear like this. Especially in light of what's going on at home this evening."

"Well, that girl sure has a mind of her own, doesn't she? Like I told you, Fran does buy groceries here quite often. If she comes in, I'll give her your message to hurry home."

"Okay. Thanks, Leann. And remember, we *are* dealing with Fran Millwright. Call me if she gives you any trouble."

"Thanks for the warning. Will do. I promise."

Eventually the office clock showed nine-fifteen, and Fran allowed herself to stand and stretch to relieve her stiff muscles. Leann came back to the office, cash drawer in hand, and flipped on the office light, having locked the front door and extinguished all other store lighting.

"Had enough of my little holding cell?"

Fran blinked in the light. "Yes. I have. But it beats being anywhere else around here under present circumstances."

"Well, at this juncture our best course of action is to get you out of town to a place of safety, and to where we can get the help we need. I've got a plan. Just do everything that I tell you."

Leann propped open the back door of the building. Her sedan sat parked nearby, and she made three trips back and forth between the building and her car, loading up miscellaneous supplies, including a few boxes of truffles.

During Leann's second trip to the car, a second, crouching figure followed her across the short interval of asphalt and slipped into the back seat.

"Stay down!" Leann hissed. She walked back to the building, pushed the back door shut, and locked it. Then returned, started the car, and pulled out and onto the road.

"Fran, we're going to assume that the sheriff and his deputies and who-knows-who-else are cruising the streets on the lookout for you. So, keep your head low until I tell you that you can sit up."

"Okay." Fran's voice was muffled from where she lay on her side, hidden under the length of Leann's dry-cleaned winter coat.

Leann steered toward a residential section on the north end of town and straight to her home, pulling directly into the garage and lowering the door.

"Okay, you can get up." She leaned over the back seat. "We're safely at my house."

Fran raised up and climbed out. Leann, leading the way and without turning on any house lights, ushered Fran from the garage into her family room. There she turned on one low table lamp. Then she moved about the house, closing the drapes in the front room.

"The Sheriff knows my routine, that I come straight home after closing up each night. For that reason, we'll hang out here awhile. I'll get you something to eat, and you can use the bathroom. Then, when I feel like the coast is clear, we'll head out."

"Sounds good. I owe you one, big time, Leann. If it wasn't for your help, I don't know what I'd do."

"Oh, you'd think of something. You're smarter than most everybody else around here. But it will be much better this way."

An hour passed. They ate a light supper, and Leann loaded the dishwasher. "It's after eleven. I know that the law around here generally meet at the all-night diner for coffee and debriefing at eleven.

This is our best chance to get out of town unnoticed." She wiped her hands on a towel and picked up her purse.

Five minutes later, Leann's car backed out of the driveway and headed out toward the highway on the north end of town, Fran once again curled up beneath a pile of clothing in the back seat.

"Oh, rats!" Leann muttered.

"What is it?"

"Oh, wouldn't you know it. I can see the sheriff, sitting right there along the main road. He knows my car. If he sees me leaving town this time of night, he'll chase me down."

"Has he spotted you?"

"No. And we won't let him."

She swung into another residential street and proceeded to the south and west, eventually turning on to another highway, proceeding due west.

"What're you doing?" Fran raised up just enough to see that everything in front of them was dark; they were outside of town.

"We're taking an alternate route. The sheriff can't be in two places at the same time."

"Where are we going?"

"To Cedarfield."

The lights of Thistle Junction faded behind Leann's car, and Fran arose and stretched. "You said we're going to Cedarfield? Why there?"

"Because it's a safe place for you. They've got a hotel, and they've got a police department that I know and trust."

"But I thought Cedarfield was a wild place. I've heard stories."

"Yes, that place does have its share of drama. But the police chief there and I are close friends. He will help us."

"That's fine. But what do we tell them? They won't understand our situation."

"I haven't decided yet. But we can at least sound an alarm. And I brought along the unopened boxes of truffles. When they see what's inside, the investigative ball gets rolling. That should bring any other issues to light."

"Whew! Things have heated up in a hurry. Who could have guessed that my asking questions could put me in such a fix? Now you, too. You've become my accomplice, at risk of becoming a target yourself."

"Yes. And, in the words of Maxwell Smart, 'loving it.'"

"But why? What's in this for you?"

"For me, justice served. Crooked city leaders and others in power need to be brought to justice, especially if innocent lives could be impacted. I care about you and enough about Thistle Junction to try to make it a better place to live. If you hadn't stepped up the way you have, I may not have been brave enough to take things on by myself."

Another hour of driving and a faint glow appeared in the sky ahead: the lights of Cedarfield. A brightly lit billboard came into view. "Escape to Paradise" in bold lettering, the image of palm trees, white sands, and blue-green waters. And the name and phone number of a local travel agency.

"How appropriate." Fran smiled at the sight. "That's what I call a good sign."

As they approached the city, Leann swung off the highway, made a couple of turns, and pulled up to the curb in front of a low brick building one block off Main Street.

"We've arrived. Police headquarters."

"You drove right to it. How did you know?"

"Like I told you, I know people here."

"Please explain—before we go inside."

"Okay." Leann shut off the engine. "From years back when I first came out to handle my uncle's affairs. I had to go all the way to Eden Prairie to find a good attorney; good legal help is hard to come by in Thistle Junction."

"No kidding."

"That's where I met Art Friedrich, at that time a police lieutenant in Eden Prairie and a close friend of my attorney. Shortly after that, Art moved to Cedarfield to become Chief of Police. We've kept in touch ever since."

"How about that? So…" Curiosity overtook Fran's reluctance to pry. "Were you and Art—how shall I say this—a couple?"

"Hmm. Yes, we were, for a while anyway. But the important thing is that we have sustained a good friendship for several years. We still get together socially on occasion."

"And tonight, we're calling on him for help."

"Yes. Art probably won't be here tonight, but I know several of his officers. I can at least introduce you and lend the credibility of my good name. Everybody knows who I am. Then we'll get you into a hotel for the night. Here." Leann stuffed a wad of currency into Fran's hand. "You'll need some spending money."

"Thanks. But what about you?"

"Unfortunately, I'll have to leave you here and drive back home tonight. I need to be back at my store tomorrow morning, just like nothing ever happened."

"And me?"

"That's where my ability to form and maintain healthy, long-term working relationships pays off. I feel confident leaving you with the authorities here for the time being. We'll have one of the officers call your parents tonight to let them know that you're safe, in their 'custody.'"

"Fine, but if anyone back home finds out you drove me up here, you'll be in a world of trouble."

"Oh, not so much. Don't forget that you're an adult. How you got up here isn't anyone else's business, and we haven't broken any laws. And, if you were paying attention, I didn't even have to lie to Sheriff Avery back at the store tonight."

"Okay, Leann." Then she remembered her friend. "Hey, be sure to keep Tony's name out of everything. He still has to live there and plans to keep working at the plant, at least through the summer."

"No problem."

"It's funny. I looked forward to my eighteenth birthday, but I hadn't anticipated everything that came along with that. Especially the new risks."

"Don't worry so much about that crew. You shouldn't have any more issues with them. When they realize that you're in the so-called custody of the Cedarfield authorities, along with a couple D-stamped boxes of Thistle Junction Truffles, I have a feeling that the gang there will be laying low. I don't expect them to bother either of us."

They climbed out of the car and walked up to the front door, where Leann pressed a buzzer. A young officer behind a desk let them in. Despite her current feelings of anxiety, Fran immediately felt drawn to the man—his broad shoulders, bright eyes, and a warm smile.

"Good evening, ladies. Ben Collig at your service."

"Hi Ben, I'm Leann Schoenheider."

"Oh, Leann! I remember. Good to see you." Collig pointed across the reception area. "Please, let's sit down. Who is your friend?"

"This is Fran Millwright, a good friend of mine from Thistle Junction. We're in need of your help."

"I'm not surprised, your showing up here after midnight and all."

For the next half-hour, Leann gave Collig an account of their situation and their suspicions. Fran found herself watching the young officer closely, admiring his gentle, yet professional manner.

At length, Leann stood and turned to Fran. "I'm going to take you to Cedarfield's one hotel. Tomorrow morning either Officer Collig or Chief Friedrich will look after you. Everything will work out."

Fran again glanced at Collig and agreed with her friend that everything would be okay. Even more than okay. Somehow, she knew it.

Matthew 5:10 (KJV)
Blessed are they which are persecuted for righteousness' sake: for theirs is the kingdom of heaven.

Matthew 5:10 (AMP)
Blessed [comforted by inner peace and God's love] are those who are persecuted for doing that which is morally right, for theirs is the kingdom of heaven [both now and forever].

Matthew 5:10 (MSG)
You're blessed when your commitment to God provokes persecution. The persecution drives you even deeper into God's kingdom.

9 798888 590478